NYMPH IN NEED

NYMPH IN NEED

JOHN B. THOMPSON

CUTTING EDGE

ISBN-13: 978-1-970848-08-3

Published by
Cutting Edge Books
PO Box 8212
Calabasas, CA 91372
www.cuttingedgebooks.com

CHAPTER ONE

Taretown is not an unusual town. Exhuberant happy writers say many such towns decorate the face of the United States. Cynical writers say they infect the same face. Taretown is no different from any other town of five thousand inhabitants when taken in the broad sense, with the possible exception of a growing plastics industry drawn there by a generally unenlightened, therefore trouble-free, labor force. Also a drawing point was the abundance of fresh water supplied by Big Bone River, remarkably free according to chemists, of numerous corrosive salts, a condition not to be found in a stream serving a greater watershed.

Taretown has one small department store, several general merchandise stores, a beauty shop, two barber shops, two drug stores, five doctors, too many lawyers, Ford Agency, Chevrolet Agency and a Dodge-Plymouth Agency. There are too many service stations and too few really good ones. There is one very good restaurant, one fair one, and a third who pays a great deal more attention to the toothsomeness and implied availability of its waitresses than its food. There are several Protestant Churches and one Catholic Church. There is a large high school that serves not only the town, but the surrounding farming community as well.

That is Taretown at a glance. Beneath cursory examination runs any number of deep muscular undercurrents affecting individuals more directly and profoundly than the town as a whole.

John Sidney Grahame, pronounced as though there was no "e", stood on a dimly lit corner on a back street and listened to the night noises. He was a well knit lad of nineteen maybe five feet, ten, weighing one hundred seventy pounds. His body was lithe, muscular, a little better than that upon close examination. His head was rather noble in cast that went well with the loping waves in his dark hair, and the quiet but classic mould of his face. His eyes were slumberous, a feral green in color, but again on close examination they revealed changing lights in their depths and a suggestion that they did not slumber at all, but were far and all-seeing.

John Sidney Grahame was a solitary soul, neither seeking nor particularly enjoying the company of boys his own age, a matter that was to be a considerable factor in his future. John Sidney Grahame by his reticense, his quiet effacing attitude that was not reflected in the noble cut of his head or the way he held it, high and without shyness, or the almost physically felt directness of his eyes, was an enigma and few people like enigmas. Enigmas always manage to take subconscious advantage of other peoples' weaknesses ... make them suspect enigmas of deep, treacherous, disloyal thoughts and strategems. Enigmas make people uncomfortable.

He leaned back against a large pen oak that stood in the corner of Dr. Hatcher's yard and listened to the night noises. The distant hum of the plastics plant, an occasional tooted car horn, the shriek of tires turning a corner too fast. The mournful blast of the crack Silver Bullet as it hurtled through the night bearing down on Taretown, haughtily ignoring it, rushing on through with undiminished speed to stop at Followell, fifty miles distant. The Silver Bullet had no time for such places as Taretown, hammering out it's disdain on gleaming rails of steel.

Far down the dim street John Sidney could see the slight figure of a girl walking fast. A baby sitter from the better section no doubt. It was twelve thirty, about the time to expect a baby sitter to be walking home if the people she sat for didn't think enough of her to take her home in the car. John Sidney sniffled the cool night air and allowed a twitt of annoyance to touch his face. Taretown was certainly no place for a girl to be walking home so late at night. Lately there had been some unpleasant things happening to women at night ... and this woman was obviously very young. She was a block away now, and John Sidney's vision, abnormally acute, caught movement in the darkness about fifty feet away in the densely grown yard of an abandoned house. It was no more than a suggestion of movement, but it brought him straight and tense. He melted into the shadows like a creature of the night ... which he was. John Sidney was a silent solitary wanderer in the night, in the woods and fields. He was a child of nature and in the embrace of her many arms he felt safe and at home.

The girl passed beneath the dim street light and he could see the rich copper-red hues of her hair in its mean illumination. She was immaturely slender, but she had either trained out or never possessed the leggy gawkiness of her age. Her step was light and graceful but hurried. She quickened her pace noticably as she passed into the dark area of the vacant house. Afraid that she would see him and be frightened, John Sidney backed into the cover of a ragged hedge growth at the edge of the sidewalk. She was now silhoutted between him and the street light. A figure, humped and soft footed, stepped quietly to the sidewalk behind her, and with a bound threw one arm about her waist and the free hand to her mouth. She struggled mightily but she was picked up like a babe and carried into the dense thicket of growth flanking the sidewalk.

They did not go alone but curiosity restrained John Sidney. His curiosity was soon satisfied. The attacker bound the girl's hands expertly with a loop of rope, still holding back any possible outcry. Then he fell on her, his free hand preparing her for a horror to which she would come so close that her mind would never be completely free of it.

The hand swept down and lifted the girl's skirt, baring her slender legs to the waist where it was splashed with a social gesture of paper thin nylon ... the same hand swept them violently from her, and the attacker fell forward, his objective almost reached.

John Sidney fascinated and curious until then, felt the searing hell of fury explode in his mind. He took two silent steps forward and encircled the man's neck from behind and tore him bodily from his victim. There were any number of things John Sidney might have done. He might have injured the man for life with a kidney punch from a knee. He might have just maintained the crushing choke hold he had on the man's neck and killed him. None of these things would have satisfied the savage discharge of adrenalin that had changed him in seconds from a quiet, curious lad into a tiger whose only thought was to rend and tear. He backed up a pace, spread his feet, evaded a backreaching, clawing hand and with all the power of his well developed shoulders, he delivered a terrible wrench that started in his own body and travelled with increasing velocity to the man he held. The force of the act lifted the man from his feet and popped him like a whip ... his neck making a sickening subdued crack. He went dead limp and John Sidney hurled him headlong into the line of bushes that bordered the sidewalk. The body crashed through them and slid almost to the street curb.

He turned to the girl who was sitting up now, trembling, her throat working with a scream that had been too long denied.

Hastily, hoping to avoid a scene that would bring screeching hysterical citizenry massing to the scene, he caught her by the shoulders and lifted her to her feet.

"It's all right now" he said in a low urgent voice.

"He won't bother you now."

She gasped, gasped again, then began to gulp air spasmodically and swing her head from side to side. John Sidney was too widely experienced to now be at a loss, and he slapped her twice, stingingly. She went rigid then collapsed against him weeping, her body convulsed and uncontrolled. He held her for a long time until she recovered and lifted her head.

"Oh ... God *Oh ... God* ..." She repeated it over and over.

"It didn't happen" he said gently. "I got here in time ... and why were you walking home?"

"How did you know ..." She became violently ill, and he held her shoulders while her tortured stomach emptied itself. He let her go to her knees and held her a long time until she regained strength. Her face and body were drenched with sweat and she shivered like she had a chill.

"They were drunk" she said, using the clean handkerchief he handed her. "Mr. and Mrs. Lerner. He couldn't drive me home and in his state I wouldn't have let him."

"I'll walk you home. Is it far?"

"No ... just around the next block, then two more. What happened to ..."

"Him ...? I broke his neck."

A vicious gleam came to her eyes. "I'm glad" she ripped out. "I'm *so* glad."

Until he had said it John Sidney hadn't actually thought so, but now he was certain. "Let's look at him" he said, a cold spot settling in the pit of his stomach.

They looked … John struck a match and the girl reeled back with a sob.

"You know him?"

She nodded distractedly. "He's Hodge Markey … son of … one of the big men at the plant … where my father works."

"Well … what do you know? Now there'll be a stink for sure."

"He goes to school … plays football … a hero …" She lifted distracted eyes. "Who are you?"

"John Sidney Grahame. Well, we'll have to tell your father and the police."

"Oh … Please … let's hurry. Don't say anything to the police … let's talk to my dad first."

"What's your name?"

"Lynn Anne Jones." They started walking.

Mr. Marvin Jones was a shocked frightened man. "Killed him you say?"

"I'm afraid so."

Mr. Jones shook his head. "Better leave it like it is. If the police get in on it, they'll naturally connect it to me … through Lynn Anne. You'd have to tell why you killed him. It wouldn't be good for you either. They'd burn you sure. I got my job to think of too."

"You mean … just let it go? Forget it?"

Mr. Jone's weak, wet face nodded eagerly. "We'd never breathe a breath of it … honest. Lynn Anne won't for sure. I sure won't. Mamma won't … will you Mamma?"

Mamma was a placid plump woman but some spirit showed through her placidity. "I guess I won't." Her lip curled. "If I hadn't lived with you through a dozen jobs a fly couldn't live off, I might feel different. Son … you ain't been here long have you?"

"No Mam. Just last week Uncle Hec and me moved here." '

"This is a town of scared men. First decent jobs they ever had, and they ain't gonna do nothing that might run 'em into danger. Police'll take orders from the plant manager. So they say. Me, I don't know. The only time I seen him he looked like a decent sort. Maybe the law just tries to figger what he wants and acts just so. Won't a thing be said and before everybody here forgets it ... you don't know who much we appreciate what you done tonight. I get sick at the stomach when I think what would have happened if you hadn't been there."

Lynn Anne crumpled over on the sofa, and began to sob wretchedly. "I wish I could tell him" she said brokenly. "I wish I could think."

Mr. Jones didn't speak. He just looked scared and embarrassed.

John Sidney got up and walked to the sofa and touched the shuddering girl on the shoulder. "I'm glad I was there, Lynn Anne. Please don't feel too badly about it."

She sat up with a jerk. "I'll never tell on you, John Sidney ... believe me, I'll never tell." Then her face went chalk white. "Oh ... My God in Heaven ... he took off my pants ... *and they're still there.*" She turned her head and fell face down on the sofa, weeping with gagging intensity.

Mr. Jones got up, his own face as pale as paper. "Guess ... I'll hafta ..."

"No" said John Sidney, standing straight. "I know exactly where to look. I'll find them. Your name on them, Lynn Anne?"

"No."

"No way to identify them?"

"They're just cheap nylons ... white," said her Mother, "Bought at Ginny's Department Store. Two for a dollar. I do my own laundry."

He nodded. "I'll fix everything."

"Maybe I'd better …"

"Not you, Pappa" said Mamma decisively. "You'd muck the thing up as sure as blazes. Take care, son, and if they've found him, let it go. They wouldn't be able to trace them to her. They had them pants on sale, and I'll bet they sold a thousand pairs."

John Sidney nodded and left the house, proceeded quietly to the scene of the attack, staying in the shadows. When he reached the yard of the abandoned house, Lynn Anne's briefs were the first thing he saw, hanging whitely from a branch. He snatched them off and approached the body cautiously. It hadn't moved. He stood in the shadows for a while thinking, then he bent over and put the garment in the body's left hand and closed the fingers on it. The body was still warm … but then it should be. On the other hand he just might be alive. John Sidney thought for a while, then turning, melted into the shadows. He found a lonely phone booth and called the police, telling them that a man was hurt on Claystone Drive in the thirteen hundred block, then hung up on their excited questions.

His house was in a poorer section of town that bordered on the Negro quarter. It was unpainted, unpretentious but had a good roof, was windproof and had a large living room which had been converted into a studio-lounge. It was unkept inside and out, but the yard grass was well trimmed and neat.

Uncle Hec was sprawled out on a threadbare sofa, scowling at a huge canvas that was nearly done. It was rampant with color … color that was indigenous to its subject which was a nude picking violets in a cozy glen. Flowers grew lushly and the woodsy setting was perfect for the blaze of color that Uncle Hec might have amplified a shade for effect. His style might have been called grand-primitive, so earthy was the overall effect. There was nothing of primitive crudeness detectable, nothing that required erudite or psychiatric explanation. The whole theme was fresh and uplifting from the water that almost provided its own sound effects to the blue jay screaming from a branch of scarlet bougainvilla. If the girl was slightly improbable, it was because beauty always did that to Uncle Hec. Her freshness was palpable, her extreme youth obvious and her detail not wanting a single strand of pubic or axillary hair. She was not a child of the civilization of storied catalogues that pass laughingly for magazines.

John Sidney came in and gave it a long look. "Something wrong?"

Uncle Hector Grahame sat up slowly. "If there is, I can't find it. That's the trouble with my stuff. It's really *good* to me. They are happy colorful daubs. I spit on sordid subjects as being worthy of art. I've had shows as I've told you. I got batted down by about every critic you can name. Some were kinder. Meloz said I had a fine sense of color ... chromatic awareness I think he called it ... One ... name of Lander, said my portrayal of depth bordered on three dimensional. Kell said I wasn't afraid of color. He seemed to think that Gaugin and I shared that one starved point in common." Uncle Hec sighed, and relaxed. He was a thick powerful man with a heavy face that was square and hard, but enjoyed soft moments. His hair was a tumbling mass of iron grey bush. His lips were sensuous and thick and his nose was high bridged and eagle beaked. He looked at John Sidney. "Been ramblin?"

"Yes Sir."

Uncle Hec turned and lay back against the sofa arm. "Almost asked you if anything happened. Nothing ever happens in this benighted hamlet except eating, sleeping, breeding and going to the bathroom."

John Sidney shook his head. "I've been thinking about that and I uncovered a lot of stuff tonight I hadn't noticed."

He gave his uncle a crisp quick rundown of the nights happenings. "I uncovered the fact that the people here are scared of the plant officials. They think they'll pull up and leave, throwing a lot of people out of work, so everyone seems to be dead determined not to do anything to harm plant-town relations. The man ... kid would be a better word, he isn't but about sixteen ... name of Markey, is the plant manager's son and the Jones' were petrified for fear it would lose Pappa his job." John Sidney's fine brows furrowed. "Times must have been pretty rough around here for everyone to be so afraid of what plant officials might think."

"Not necessarily" said Uncle Hec. "By that I mean this. Rear a boy in a small town and unless he's got considerable get up and go, he'll hang around and make any sort of precarious living just to stay home. Some can't wait until they can shake the small town dust. Others you can't make shake it.

"Maybe" said John Sidney carefully, "it's because of this fear that travels in a circle here. Their opinion I gathered to be that just because this Markey is the plant manager's son I'd get fried, no matter how justified I was and it'd mean trouble for Jones no matter if it wasn't his fault or his daughter's."

Uncle Hec nodded slowly. "Well, they could be right. Probably not as right as they think. Just the same I don't think I'd talk it around." He squared around and looked at the boy. "You sit there as cool as a plate of sherbet, tell about *murdering* a man, and you don't turn a hair."

"There's a difference between killing and murdering." The boy's eyes were somber. "And you sat there and discussed trivialities for half an hour. We're just getting around to what I did."

Uncle Hec thrust a short thick pipe into his mouth and lit it, holding it steady in his massive jaws. "Boy, you have a wide streak of your father in you. You didn't know him too well."

"No sir. He always seemed to be in and out."

"That's him. Went into World War Two, too old, then managed to make it into the Korean Police Action. Thirteen planes to his credit in the first go, and ten in the second. He went down off Inchon and we never heard from him again. Presumed lost and insurance paid." He puffed a while. "Too young to remember your mother, I suppose."

"Just vaguely. She died when I was four."

"Well, I suppose I'm a poor mother-father substitute, what with all my peculiarities."

"I have no fault to find."

"Not even when we spent half the insurance drifting around?"

"No sir."

"Not even when you had to lay out a year from high school so we wouldn't have to dig into your half saved for college?"

"No sir."

Uncle Hec grunted. "I'm not much good, boy. I'm too prone to take the easy way. I'm a good artist whom no one but the two of us thinks is good. If I'm not a good artist, then I'm good for nothing." He slewed around. "I got that itchy feeling that like your father, life is going to swirl around you like a flash flood and you'll always keep it at flood stage."

"No. I think I'm like him in some ways, but he was loaded with nervous energy. I like to waste time thinking and smelling the woods ... walking around in the cool dark damp ... like tonight."

"Just the same ... I don't know whether life came to him always in the brightest of colors or whether he found it himself, and painted it. Maybe some of both."

"Why don't we go ahead and dig into that last half of the insurance. I have one more year in high school. College ... I don't know. Maybe I'll find a way.'"

Uncle Hec shook his leonine head. "I was wrong to let us squander the first half. I'll not touch the remainder."

"But you've got to live Uncle Hec."

"Why?"

John Sidney chuckled. "As well as you love to eat and drink?"

The big man shook himself. "Boy, don't shove temptation at the old man. Always remember that he's a no good wastrel and has been living on your money for ten years."

"That timber job is good. I like it. Its' outside and in the deep woods … they're ruining the woods though."

"You didn't leave any evidence at the spot marked G?"

"No. I checked everything in my pockets. I don't smoke. Nothing's missing."

Uncle Hec sighed. "Here it is two o'clock and neither of us have slept a wink."

"That might be a good idea."

His uncle frowned. "You know something, you never were a boy. You've been grown since you were eight and before then you were too smart for your britches. Sometimes I don't know what makes you tick, then I think about your father. He ticked to beat hell for a long time and me and a lot of people never knew what sort of immortality he possessed. I can't any more picture him dead than I can fly. His sort just don't die."

"He's dead," said John Sidney slowly. "Let's go to bed."

Mike O'Boyle Taretown high school football coach hummed a tune under his breath and twirled his key chain. He was aware of the well knit youngster who sat on the sidelines nearby, but it hadn't made a conscious impression on him. As had happened on other times the chain parted and Mike cursed automatically, instantly envisaging enlisting the whole team to search for his keys. This time something startling happened. The lad near him, without any previous warning whatever, reached up and plucked the keys out of the air. It was done so smoothly that it smacked of a jugglers trick. He smiled, got up and handed it back. "Yours coach?"

"Er ... yeah ... Say, I haven't seen you around."

"I'm John Sidney Grahame. I don't go to school."

"Oh ... of course." The boy was a man ... mature. Not the age of the callow nitwits he was trying to browbeat into a team. Mike examined him as he shook hands. Not slender ... not bulky. Just right. Symmetry, that's what he had ... symmetry. Mike tasted the word and liked it. Not only that, the boy's reflexes were perfect. He could tell from the way he had picked those keys out of the air. The smooth grace with which he had poured himself off the ground as he got up to hand it back. "Ever play the game?"

"Yes sir. Some."

"What position?"

"The ends and backfield ... quarter and half."

"What system?"

"Split T, conventional T. We used a modifield single wing on some plays ... just enough to keep the opposition from knowing when a quick kick was coming."

"You kick?"

"Some."

"Like to boot a few?"

"I don't mind ... could I borrow a pair of cleats?"

"Sure, come on."

Ten minutes later John Sidney received a bad pass from the center, made a prodigious side spring to avoid two ends coming in and flat foot kicked fifty seven yards in the air. O'Boyle's jaw dropped and he bit a forefinger. "Do that again, son."

This time the pass was better and John Sidney hurled a foot into the ball with all the power of his stout right leg. The ball went slightly off to the side spiraled upward and seemed to grow small as it climbed. It struck the ground and spinning like a propeller, scooted out on the seven yard line."

"Sixty two yards coach," yelled the assistant, stepping on the line.

"You put that out of bounds on purpose?"

John Sidney shook his head. "No sir. It went off the side of my foot."

Mike mopped a perspiring forehead. "Run me a quick kick, John Sid. Put a foot in it."

They lined up in a tight single wing, John Sidney took the hard snap from the center, did a dazzling fake toward a spinner and kicked the ball straight downfield while looking at the sidelines. It went forty seven yards and rolled two more.

Mike shook his head sadly. "Son, howcome you never went to college?"

John Sidney smiled. "I haven't finished high school."

"*What*? You told me ..."

"I said I wasn't in school ... I'm not."

"Holy cow ... *holy cow*. You elegible?"

"I suppose so ... I mean my grades are all right."

O'Boyle put his hands on John Sidney's shoulder. "You're three weeks late, but we can fix that. You can enroll tomorrow."

John Sidney shook his head. "Sorry, coach. It'll be next year, maybe year after next before I go back."

The coach groaned. "Wouldn't you know it, and me with my first string quarterback injured. His mother is always on my ass howcome I don't let him carry the ball. Fact is, he can't carry it. He's scared to be tackled and that's ruination for a ball carrier. Fairly fast and got enough weight for high school but no bottom, no guts. Fair passer, good kicker ... not like you, of course, and he couldn't get a quick kick off if the opposing line fell dead. Fair to middlin' ball handler but ... the best I got. You sure you can't make it this year? If you got a financial problem we might be able to pitch in if I find an ear to talk into ... and I know a few."

John Sidney pondered a moment. "I have an uncle to take care of. Sorry. Anyhow, I couldn't take money. I have a good job in the woods. I don't take handouts."

With that Michael O'Day O'Boyle had to be content.

CHAPTER TWO

Two girls dressed themselves with the same reverent care as though both were properly respectful of what nature had done for them. In the bedroom of one, Delani Smith, there was scarcely one complete dressing of clothes ... not much to pick from. In the other, the dressing room of Patti Markey, there was enough clothes for a small army of young women. In the drawer which she now had open and was staring into with a thoughtful look was some thirty pairs of frothy undergarments. Some white and plain and designed to fit as a breathless gesture to convention, others of every color in the rainbow, designed for moods and effects. Still others had cost more than any such attire deserved what with various laces frills ... flounces and other superfluous frippery. She chose one pair of pale rose that had been threaded all over with little invisible units of elasticity which when she drew them over her lushly rounded hips, fitted her with such shocking intimacy that speaking protection-wise, she might not have had them on at all. The legs were bordered in lace so fine that a spider might have spun it and it gave her soft but sufficient thighs the air of wearing frothy halos about their upper extremities.

She straightened up and observed the effect in the full length mirror and shivered with appreciation. Patti Markey was a person of vast appreciation ... for herself. She chose a matching bra with little to recommend it except the exhorbitant price and the exquisite fit, most of which was not the fault of the bra but of what it contained. Patti was not, as they said at high school, a rack-stack. Her curves were many, elegant, generous, and as firm as one expects the very young to be. She was aware of what they did to men ... the age didn't matter a great deal ... just so they were men. Boys her own age did a great deal of ogling, whistling and eye rolling, but she could handle them too easily. Patti was still technically a virgin. She did not want to give herself. She wanted to be taken and she doubted that anyone of her acquaintance had what it took to do a salutary job of taking. Patti did not want to be brutalized or forced. What she wanted was some man to sweep her off her feet and not jump back at the first tear or the first half hearted protest. Her boy friends seemed to want a general all-around agreement before anything of a deep significance was attempted. Many had tried to entice her, many had tried to force her, but there was no guts behind their force.

Patti Markey slipped over her head a delightful creation in dusty deep rose, a summer weight knit thing that shimmered in the light of her dressing room. It fitted with the same respect to wealth and her body that her underthings had fit. She slammed a stiff brush through her minx haircut, gloated at how soft and managible it was, how it glistened as black as a crow's wing. She mussed it perversely, then put on her one concession to cosmetics, lipstick. She applied it with care and the result was all she had hoped for. She rebrushed her hair and looked at the general effect. What she saw was, an imperious, lovely girl with deep brown eyes, black hair. Her lips were full and pouty and her teeth, as she smiled at herself, were straight from a dental ad. She spun about on the balls of her feet, as light as a fawn, and tripped out of her room.

Delani Smith lived in another part of town. Her house was old and rather moth eaten, but it was comfortable. Delani's room was one she shared with three sisters ... not real sisters, but children of her foster mother.

Delani was darkly tanned, and as she stood before her wavy spotted mirror she too was properly proud of what she saw. She was as slim and sinewy as a greyhound with a soft overlay of rounding tissue that kept her muscularity from being a liability. She was as finely conditioned as a racer and her face was alive, alert and bright. Her hair was a waterfall of silken black wonder, heavy and thick. She always did it up by parting it in the middle and making two buns that nestled back of her tiny shapely ears. Her eyes were the deepest blue which shone startingly from her nut-brown face that had been so delightfully conditioned by the sun that one almost always thought of some foreign blood. Filipino, Latin American ... or in the case of Taretown ... Negro.

She slid her feet through the legs of her briefs ... plain white, cheap rayon and pulled them up smoothing out the wrinkles until they lost the manifest cheapness of their purchase price when filled with the symphonic lines of her middle. Her breasts, high prominent, as firm as quinces were tipped with the most delicate pink and as she had many another time, because she had no bra, put on her dress without any support for them. They needed no support, but the exciting erections they made in the front of her dress suggested that they might have needed some restraint.

Delani was not dressing for male companions. Mostly she was afraid of them because they all seemed to want the same thing. No matter what the color of their skins. White boys wanted her because they considered her colored, therefore, fair game. Colored boys wanted her because she was light of skin and had "good hair." They were more respectful, but at the same time, more insistent. White boys were crude, rude and objective. Colored boys were sly, eager, just as objective in mind but less obvious in intent. Delani's oldest sister was a school teacher and the care of the other four children fell to their mother, a plump, happy, efficient widow. They called her Mamma Dell.

Mamma Dell had gotten the three oldest together one day and had told them in blunt yoeman language what every man was after, how he expected to acquire it and what it would mean to them as individuals. She did not try to frighten them, but she gave it to them as ungarnished as a boiled potato. She explained the pitfalls and how to avoid them and Mamma Dell knew because she was a renowned midwife who had delivered babies in the tens of hundreds, whose services had been in such demand by the doctors that when Mamma Dell began to grow too plump to walk long distances, they would send for her in their automobiles. To keep up with progress one doctor insisted that she take a course in midwifery. There were those who thought Mamma Dell's modest background was such that she might not make it, but she fooled them all by taking a stringent night course in the three R's and making it the rest of the way by sheer "mother-wit." She emerged with honors, her instructors a little groggy from what *they* had learned while teaching Mamma Dell.

Dr. Joe Hamilton, the one who had insisted that Mamma Dell take the course discussed her with an instructor. "She" said the woman with profound respect, "showed us a new wrinkle in mouth to mouth artificial respiration. The point is, she knew about the technique a long time before it was written up. There are a few other things she knows too ... that I didn't expect. In fact, I find myself wishing I had all her tricks ... such as ..." The woman shrugged. "That was one I didn't catch. She reversed a breech the other day that had us buffaloed ... it smacked of magic."

"Experience," said the plump doctor, with a grin. "I'd rather have her on a difficult delivery than anyone I know."

Delani slipped on her cheap print dress which fitted in a manner that made the price of the garment difficult to consider. She grinned and whirled around watching the hem as it flared upward and showed her slim but lushly sculptured thighs. She sat down and began to apply her lipstick, like Patti Markey, it was her only concession to synthesis. She touched a fingertip with her tongue, smoothed down her thick swallow winged brows and sat back. Her face was pure oval, but her eyes seemed slightly slanted because of their almond shape. They were large, expressive and melting ... seemed always to be slightly dampened as from recent tears. This fact had made many a man catch his breath ... not to know why. Some it annoyed because a mere colored girl is not supposed to cause any sort of emotional upheaval in a white man.

Some kept their emotions to themselves and hoped. Some hated her and allowed as to how one day they'd get her, the stuck-up, this, that and the other ... loudly, stridently they said it thereby making themselves obvious. Not infrequently she heard them and she'd quicken her step and her heart would pound heavily.

It was inevitable that she should dream of men. White men more often than not, because her own skin was so light, because any minority is likely to look toward the direction they consider up rather than the reverse. Because Mamma Dell had hinted several times that it was more than a bare possibility that Delani was really white ... not that Delani believed her. It seemed too much for belief and what good was it? She was thought of as colored and that was that ... in Taretown, at any rate. Mamma Dell had brought Delani to be a part of the household when, as Mamma Dell said ... "Her string wasn't dry yet." Mamma Dell had always been somewhat chary about the details of how she acquired the girl and no one had ever pressed her about it.

Carla, Mamma Dell's oldest daughter was a houri in bronze, a large woman in that she was tall, statuesque. She had a good education and her husband had been principal of the colored school until his death from a heart condition. Carla had continued to teach to support the family and Mamma Dell, who, with age creeping upon her, had gone into semi-retirement to care for the household. On special cases Dr. Hamilton could get her help, but most of the time she stayed home, cooked, cleaned house, and kept an eagle eye on her charges.

Delani ... as a name was the brainchild of Mamma Dell. She discarded all of the common ones as too conventional. The child must have a better name and Mamma Dell, after much deliberation and laborious scrawling to see what came out of various letter combinations, decided upon Delani as the name of choice. She had never heard of it before nor had the many people she questioned about it before deciding.

Delani, as trim as a filly colt and twice as fractious, tripped out to the front porch where her step-sister Rose waited. "You sure took your time," said Rose acidly. She wasn't quite jealous of Delani, but enough so to annoy Mamma Dell who was always on the lookout for some sign of it.

"Time," said Mamma Dell, "is the thief of mankind. Nobody's going to do you outa your share so you better use it. When your time comes it'll steal you just like it's stole people since Adam and Eve. Go back in there and put on clean socks. People's think I don't keep you in clo'se."

Rose pouted because it was the only safe retaliation she could think of at the moment, but she went back and changed her socks.

"It's Sunday night," said Mamma Dell. "Y'all don't fool around none after the show.

Delani, nearly eighteen, and Rose fourteen walked away primly, each conscious that as long as Mamma Dell could see them they'd better act *like ladies.*

Patti Markey left her home on the swankier side of town in a convertible driven by a young blood who promised to have her back at eleven. They were supposed to go to Church, but instead they'd secretly arranged to attend a club of the shadier sort in the next county.

Jack Develin was cut from the usual mould and Patti arrived home ... on time and in a foaming rage

In her room Patti tossed her garments off with faint respect for their richness and glowered at her pink body in the mirror.

She could feel the heat of his lips on hers, the tingling trails left by his questing hands. Her bra had come off easily because he had managed to loosen it. Her breasts were pink and excited and rich disturbed blood hammered at her temples with slow solid blows. She knew what had happened to Jack. It had happened before. In a fevered fury she had slapped him until his ears rang and his pride was prostrate before her.

"You can take me home now ... you ... *child,*" she had said with withering scorn.

Crushed, he had done as she asked. She sat down and brushed her hair with a fury that soon had it crackling with electricity and standing out in fine silken order. She paused and wondered why both parents had been home when she came in. One should be at the hospital with her brother Hodge who had been found in a critical condition in front of an empty house, his neck badly dislocated. He must be better. She was glad. She was faced with the sisterly necessity of visiting him, but she hated him and didn't want to go.

Delani and Rose walked slowly home from the movie, their spirits undiminished by the morbid nature of the show that had had a terrible ending.

Once home Rose went straight to bed, but Delani was restless. She changed to a pair of faded blue shorts that had been jeans once. She put on the top of a shortie pajama set that did little but fog the leaping revolt of her breasts, and stepped off the back porch.

Mamma Dell put her head out of the kitchen. "Where you goin' chile," she asked.

"Just thought I'd walk back here on the ravine."

"All right, but don't go far in that get up. Might be some men trompin' around in that gully."

The ravine ran directly behind the house. Just across it was another house backed up to it. It had been vacant for a long time, but several months ago two men, one old and one young had moved in. Delani had watched them ... the young man especially, because he was young and to Delani outrageously handsome. He was quiet and restrained, not like others his age.

She found an old milk can and putting it mouth-down against an oak tree and sat leaning back against the hole.

Norman McLeod, newspaper reporter had been with the police when they picked up Hodge Markey. He had observed and taken pictures of the scene, the popping of police bulbs effectively camouflaging his own. Before they could warn him against taking pictures he had what he wanted and they were none the wiser.

He presented his pictures and copy in time for the morning edition of the Taretown Chronicle only to have it shoved rudely back. "We won't publish a line of this," said the man at the desk. McLeod, tall, tough and mean, lipped a cigarette into the opposite corner of his mouth. "Howcome? It's written from on the scene observation. The pictures support the story."

"That's not the point. The boy there is the son of Judson Markey."

McLeod shrugged and pushed his hat back on his mahogany red hair. "What the hell do I care whose son he is. Think of it. Hodge Markey ... in trouble three times already for similar offenses and now some pullet breaks his neck. Have you no sense of poetic justice? Have you no imagination? Think, if you will, of a chick ... maybe a hundred pounds or so breaking her attacker's neck *after* said attacker has possessed himself of her underthings."

"The story," said the editor offensively, "gets printed ... the way the boy was found, where and by whom. No mention will be made of the underthings. No speculations will be made as to how his neck got broken. Nothing will be said of past transgressions, and no pictures."

McLeod slitted his eyes against cigarette smoke. "What sort of rag is this you're running? Whose phoot are you kissing, and why?

Kurt Marx had gone purple. "I like my job," he ground out with slow emphasis. "I take orders and by God, as long as you work for this paper you'll take orders."

McLeod laughed nastily. "You silly bastard. What the hell do I care about this crummy rag?" He leaned forward, "Son, I got some lousy news for you. This town, because you print a rag instead of a newspaper, subscribes to and buys from the stands three out-of-town newspapers. The *Daily Advocate* of Bloomington will be tickled pink to get my story with pictures. It'll hit the stands exactly four hours after your does." He stood straight, his eyes reckless, his lips sour with sarcasm. "You can't fire me. You didn't hire me and before I go I'll have a good strong talk with the only man on the staff here who can. Good day, Pansy."

He left Kurt Maryx in a plum colored rage, carrying his pictures and copy with him. The paper would carry the police report buried on page four. This he knew, he knew also that considerable dust would fly when the story came out over the wires as it most likely would when he sent it in to the *Daily Advocate* of Bloomington.

Although it didn't make the predicted edition, it made the Monday morning product and the smoke and dust began to lift as Norm McLeod had predicted. Some enterprising copy man had inserted an eyecatching headline. "Girl Bites Hound." Norm's opening sentence carried on the theme. "Worms turn and cornered rats fight, as one young man of Taretown can now attest. Having come to the notice of the police three times before and reaping nothing more damaging than a slap on the wrist, our midnight Casanova, one Hodge Markey, caught a tartar last Saturday night. Said tartar must have been of the old breed because Hodge's prize was nothing more exciting than a pair of frothy underpants, for which he almost paid the extreme price. When discovered he was in a state of unconsciousness which passed when surgeons with great care reduced a dislocated cervical vertebra. It is not thought that Markey will be permanently injured but his fair victor could hardly have been certain of that when she gave him a *Karate* chop ... or whatever means she used to so effectively unjoint his neck."

There was a great deal more but few citizens, most of whom had been aware of Markey's exploits, invariably with daughters of men whose livelihood depended on the jobs they held with the company were inclined to read further. They were sore, but still silent.

Judson Markey was a hard working man with too many troubles directly related to his job for him to borrow any at home. Moreover, his wife Esther provided a certain uncommon air of capability accompanying less than the required minimum of talent. This she accomplished by glib recitations which she memorized from women's magazines written by men for the female trade in which they were careful not to say anything that might offend their customers. From such sources sprang the wisdom of Esther Markey who clove to the let-'em-alone school which exposes the premise that growing youngsters should be given almost limitless latitude so that their psyches will not be traumatized ... this in the face of the axiom that children are geniuses at broadening their own latitude with neither help nor hindrance of their parents. Thus Patti felt quite without shame in pursuing the dictates of her glands with the bland and guiltless indifference of a woman whose respect for such inconsequentials as morals or conscience is long past.

Hodge, a handsome muscular youth was much in demand by the daughters of lesser men, namely, men subordinate to his father. They found him irresistible, but this was pale pap for him to exist on. Hodge had long since become jaded, fed up with the soft white bodies he found to be his for the pleasure of his company. That his attraction was something less than unanimous goes without saying and to those who found no thrill in his touch went his interest. They not only were not thrilled when he asked for a date ... something that irked him out of countenance, some were actively offensive about it. There had been Constance O'Boyle, the coach's daughter, Althea Hardy, the daughter of a local merchant, Belle North, daughter of the local mortician, and lastly Lynne Anne Jones. Lynne Ann had two points that distinguished her from the others. Though the others had succumbed to his strength and the solitude of their tryst, they were not directly beholden to Hodge through his father and theirs. Hodge didn't recall what had happened except that he had been lifted from Lynne Anne's body like a sack of straw and popped like a whip. After that there was a large black balloon of darkness where he had remained until the surgeons skillfully put the joint back in place. Hodge was now in excruciating traction unable to move his head, and therefore able to ponder greatly and wonder. He knew that Lynne Anne had certainly not had a hand in his accident. He did not as yet know that the newspapers were taking the attitude that she had ... with a vengeance.

CHAPTER THREE

Delani sat on the milk can and listened to the whisper and hum of the night. It was warm so she had unbuttoned the pajama jacket she wore and the edges of the garment fell apart hanging percariously onto the petal smooth swells of her breasts.

John Sidney had gotten quite close before he realized that she didn't know he was present. She was softly revealed in the reflection of two street lights that filtered illumination through the branches of the larger trees. She was breath taking. Her face was a calm quiet study, her body was a poem of youthful symmetry. If nature had outdone herself in certain spots it is because nature knows how to attract and she habitually favors some of her children over others. His eyes saw the dim cleft between her breasts, the exciting creaminess of her flawless skin, the stygian gleam of her thick hair. There was something ethereal about her face that seemed to cover a banked fire, a slumbering volcano that could burst into flame. He shuddered at his own thoughts, swallowing back the sickness that had stayed at the pit of his stomach since he knew he had killed a man. At the moment the sight of Delani threatened to make him forget that he had.

He went so far out of himself as to step on a stick that snapped alarmingly in the quiet and brought the girl to her feet with a smooth quick movement.

He knew he should speak while fright was still on her or she'd be frightened all over again if he waited. "I'm sorry if I scared you," he said in a soft apologetic voice.

To his surprise she relaxed, smiled and closed her pajama top with a smooth movement. "I guess I must have jumped a foot. I didn't see you."

He walked up to her and saw the thinness of the garment she wore, the tight fit of the shorts, and her concern for keeping an arm across her breasts.

"I walk a lot in the night … in the woods and fields. I walk quietly because you see more that way." He stopped and reddened from embarrassment.

She laughed ringingly. "I'll say you do. I must have looked like I was ready for a raw swim a moment ago …" She blushed in turn and it made her eyes brilliant.

"I'm sorry," he said so contritely that her throat grew warm and thick with a wonderful feeling.

"I didn't mean to spy but …" He sighed, held his palms up in a token of surrender. "I couldn't help it. You're the most beautiful person I ever saw."

She gasped and held her pajama top with fierce strength. Her eyes widened, her lips parted and her breath staggered from the overload of emotion it carried. "You …" Tears started from her eyes and coursed down her cheeks making golden rivulets that caught the soft light.

A raging pain struck John Sidney in the chest. He stepped closed and touched her shoulders with his fingertips. "I didn't mean any harm. I didn't mean to make you cry … Please don't cry."

The tears flowed faster but a bubble of laughter came to the girl's lips. "You didn't make me cry … that is … it was just what you said … the way you said it. You *must* mean it."

John Sidney was stopped cold. "Of *course* I mean it."

Her lips worked and her breath came faster. Her arm dropped away from the proud peaks of her breasts. Their form and breathless sharpness came to him from his angle of vision. His heart hammered so loudly that he could feel the beats physically. For a long moment they both endured a period of cataclysmic upheaval … an upheaval that would calm but never leave them again as long as they lived.

"I'm … Delani Smith." Her eyes begged him, her lips entreated him, her whole being was humbled before him.

John Sidney shivered in the grip of something very like religious terror. This was not real. It was not true. "I'm … John Sidney Grahame."

"I've seen you …"

She gasped for breath for a moment then a feeling of fright, of something she had never known before, a fear of the future, a million fears she could not define … overlaid with a wave of desire that stunned her. Not desire as she was to know it later but desire to be someone, to mean something to this man who was stupified at the sight of her, who so palpably wanted her to be a part of him. The limits of her endurance was reached. Her mind could not function properly and in the midst of this chaos an overpowering impulse struck her. With a sinuous movement she was in his arms, her lips searched and found his, clung with a sweetness that made John Sidney's mind erupt in a roar of reaction. His arms imprisoned her but the impulse that had made her act also contained the element of flight. He had aborted that portion of it. She went as tense as a tight wire, resisting the savagery that had shattered the kiss into an opening of portals where one searched for the soul of the other. Her tenseness fled before the onslought of a weakness she had never felt before. A cry sounded in the distant reaches of her throat … but the pressure of his lips and his desperate searching for the ultimate magic of her mouth prevented it reaching the surface. Her breasts against his chest were like twin points of searing flame, erect, hard, palpitant and throbbing to the pounding cadence set up by her racing heart.

Her strength returned and she tore away and fled as though pursued by witches.

John Sidney sank to his knees, hammered down by the awful power of something new to him. Something he could not have forseen. She was not a person now, she was divinity. In all his years he had never suffered such a blow. There had been emotional upheavals. Even the darker hues of a more mature sort of love was not a stranger to John Sidney, but none of them had ever been accompanied by such blasting ecstasy that his mind refused to function ... his body now weak and trembling overcome by the fearful spray of adrenalin that had sprung through him ... just as the rage had possessed him when he saw Lynn Anne Jones about to be brutally ravished ... only that time there had been a maniacal strength not weakness.

For a long time he remained in kneeling position, then slowly he got up and retraced his steps back to the house where he found Uncle Hec deep into a fifth of gin, frowning heavily at the now finished painting.

"What's wrong with it," asked John Sidney conventionally.

"It's finished," snorted Uncle Hec, brandishing the bottle. "This is the time all artists, not commercial hacks, fear, although I've been called a commercial hack, a draftsman and I don't know what all. They and I fear the end because it either falls and stands when it is finished, John Sidney, while I quaff this colorless nectar that ravels up the sleeve of care, sit there and tell me what's wrong with it."

"I'm not a critic, Uncle Hec."

"Neither, dammit, are the critics.

John Sidney examined the canvas minutely.

"If you will notice," said Uncle Hec wiping his mouth, depositing the bottle carefully on the floor, "my birds look like birds. My flowers look like flowers. My woman looks like a woman ... a mighty fine hunk of woman, mind you, but she's a woman. Her fingers aren't sticks of dirty wood, her face isn't the square lifeless face of a sow with holes for eyes. Her breasts aren't pendulous obscenities."

"All I can tell you," said John Sidney carefully, "is that I like it. It appeals to my senses, it is colorful, it is true to detail. What else should a painting have?"

Uncle Hec laughed caustically. "Just about anything but what you've mentioned. I don't know why. I don't know why so strongly that I couldn't paint one of those obscure excrescences I've seen called 'the only true art,' if my life depended on it. Art to me is the reproduction of something on canvas. 'That's the way I see it' one beaded maniac told me once. I replied that if that was the way he saw it, I'd hate like hell to send him to the market for a sirloin steak. He was offended and said as much in rather abusive langauge."

"What'd you do?"

"I clobbered him one right in the middle of his beard. Some screeching female tried to claw my eyes out. She needed a bath the worst way."

When the thought struck him John Sidney's vision went dim from the force of it and it took him some time to recover from it. Uncle Hec was aware that it had happened before the boy turned around.

If ... you can paint *her* ..." He gasped for breath. "If you can paint *her* in the *nude* ... like you did this one here ... if you can see and feel and know what she is then you'll be hung in the Louvre."

Uncle Hec sat up slowly. He knew his nephew too well to treat the statement lightly. "Tell me boy."

John Sidney told him as he always told everything without embellishment with merciless objectivity.

Uncle Hec pondered for a long time after John Sidney had stopped talking. "Tonight, you said?"

"Just before I came in here."

"I felt it. To much gin to see it. I felt it … like the heat from an invisible fire." Uncle Hec smiled wearily. "She'd scream and run. So many do. A really *good* model is a rare creature to find. A very rare creature."

John Sidney pondered. "It's too soon for me to say. I don't know. Maybe she would and maybe she wouldn't." He lifted his somber grey eyes. "There's just one thing. If it's what I expect, I won't let it be sold."

Uncle Hec shivered and wondered why he did. "Son … from what you tell me, she's colored."

John Sidney's back straightened. "I don't care if she's a Fiji head hunter."

"I rather suspected that to be the case." The old man sighed. "Ah well … suppose we go to bed. That settles most questions temporarily."

CHAPTER FOUR

Monday morning was a day all of Taretown would remember, but most of its citizens would have liked to forget it.

Mr. Judson Markey, hard at work trying to sort out from a pile of suggestions, some new and remunerative uses for Markite his most promising plastic, was perked from concentration by Miss Walker, his secretary. "Mrs. Markey is on the phone and she seems upset."

He sighed. When Esther was upset she had a perfect genius for communicating the infection to others. He had grown relatively but not entirely immune. He lifted the receiver. "Yes, Esther."

"Judson … the most awful thing has happened. You must come home this instant. I can't talk about it over the phone."

He frowned. "Is Hodge worse?"

"No … Hodge is doing fine, Dr. Forrest says. It's something else entirely. You'd better bring Whitley with you."

Mr. Markey's breath shut off suddenly. If she wanted the plant attorney then something must indeed be wrong. He spoke a few more words then hung up.

"Miss Walker don't disturb these suggestions. Some of them are quite practical. I'll go into them further when I come back."

"At what time sir … in case someone wants to know?"

"Tell them you don't know."

He was a busy, harrassed man upon whom the conviction had been creeping for some time that he was burning too much of the candle, too fast.

Whitley was a thin, tall intense young man who worked hard and was not enchanted at being called away from an important paper he was working on. Whitley like most successful lawyers was quite vocal and possibly not as respectful as he might have been. "What'n hell does she want at eleven in the morning?"

"That's what we're going to find out."

"Well ... what does she need me for?"

"I'm sure I don't know," said Mr. Markey shortly. "She said to bring you."

Whitley sighed. "You know Jud, seven years ago when we started this plant it was fun. Now it's become a rat race. It's telling on you too. You've got bags and lines you didn't have when you came here."

"I know," said Markey, still short. He knew the strain was telling on him, but he didn't care to be reminded about it. They drove up to the lovely functional house with its glass brick, glass panels, natural stone and impeccable yard.

Markey led the way into the living room, a husky ex-athlete whose clothes were beginning to look baggy because he had held himself well when they were fitted, then slumped afterward. His stiff hair was a corn tassel blonde still worn in a modified crew-cut. His amber eyes were tired and somewhat sunken.

Esther met him in the living room in a housecoat that cost a pretty penny but did little to soften her angular shape. Her face was starved but well tended and might have been pretty at one time. Markey could recall the lovely well fleshed woman he had married, but that was before she had tried every diet she could find in her magazines.

"What's the trouble now," he inquired bluntly.

"Read this," she said dramatically, thrusting out a newspaper which he saw to be the *Daily Advocate*.

"Whitley, will you have coffee?"

"Thanks, no. I had too much at the plant."

Markey read the article, looked at the pictures and handed it back to his wife. "Well ...?"

"*Well*. Is that all you have to say?"

"I recall saying a few things when he was in trouble before. I recall further that you advised silence. I was stupid, so I was silent. Now this. What shall I do, sue the editor?"

"That's exactly why I asked you to bring Whitley. Whitley, read this. I want them sued for a million dollars ... I want them put out of business. I want them ruined and driven to poverty. The very idea of maligning my dear son like this. It's just another spoke in the wheel to villify him, to hurt him by these people who are jealous of his popularity ... who're jealous of his athletic ability. People who hate him and want to hurt him. I'll not stand idly by and see it happen either. Not me. I'm not made of that sort of metal. It all started when that little bitch of an O'Boyle girl told that awful tale on Hodge, then it was that North *thing* ..."

Whitley handed her the paper back. "I'm afraid I don't know what you're talking about, Mrs. Markey."

"Indeed. Judson, tell him what *I'm* talking about"

Markey felt numb. He was miserably tired and something very like indigestion began to boil up inside him. "I'm afraid I don't know what you're talking about either."

"*Judson.*" She was aghast.

He got up and lost his temper. "Have you lost your damn tongue. Why don't you *tell* us what you're talking about."

She went pale and bit her lip. "It's the vilest sort of character assassination and you mean to tell me you'll stand by and let this sort of thing be done to your own flesh and blood?"

Whitley shoved the paper at her. "Mrs. Markey, unless I'm blind this picture *is* of Hodge. Unless I'm not up on female fashions he *is* holding a pair of unmentionables in his hand Any reporter has the right to make reasonable inferences on the basis of evidence. Have no fear, there is not a single actionable line in the story. Now maybe Hodge is in the habit of carrying a pair of these things around in his hand, and while still clutching them, get his neck dislocated. I say it is possible. I've never seen a jury of dunces who would agree. He was found as you see him there. I know of McLeod. He's a reporter with a high national reputation. He's recuperating from an operation, and that's why he's here. He thinks too much of his standing in the reportorial profession to pull any sort of cute trick just to get a story."

"Do you mean to tell me that any newspaper can do this to a citizen and get away with it scot free?"

Judson Markey had a habit that had caused many a person considerable annoyance, that of making a crushing statement, then walking out with the echoes of it still ringing. "You forget one thing Esther," he said, hardness overcoming the tiredness in his voice.

"What is that?" she said, her lips almost blue.

"They haven't printed anything that isn't true. Come, Whitley."

They walked out and left her gasping and clenching her hands.

Judson Markey got in the car, waiting for Whitley to seat himself. Markey passed a shaking hand over his face. "Is a man a traitor because he refuses to feel that his son is a chip off the stone of truth?"

"No," said Whitley flatly. "What's bothering you is, what have you left undone? What made Hodge like he is?"

"You're usually right, Whit, but wrong this time. I know very well what's wrong with him. I let his mother rear him. I let her take him to a so-called psychiatrist the time he crucified the kitten to the garage. I let her handle the situation when he cut off one of Patti's toes with an axe. He was trying to cut off her foot. I let the preacher talk to him the time he dropped a little dog into the hot Sunday School stove."

"Um … you let others handle it. How would you have handled it?"

Markey lifted his shoulders. "I should have started early and none of it would have happened. If it had I'd have torn his hide from him. My father never whipped me but once, but he did such a job that it never had to be repeated. Fella … he damn near killed me."

Whitley chuckled. "I can recall a few hidings I got when I was a kid. My old man could lay it on, too, and the funny thing is, I never resented it. I suppose it was because I knew I was guilty and deserved it."

Markey nodded. "Of course, it was. I think a child expects to be punished. I think actually they subconsciously want it and are the better for it."

"And now?"

"You have my permission not to enter suit against the *Daily Advocate*."

"That's generous of you. You know what I think? I think you should take a couple of days off, get drunk and roll in the gutter until you're unrecognizable. Take two more days to recuperate, then you'll feel all unravelled and carefree. What's pressing now?"

"The suggestion box. We're beating the bushes for new ideas. I don't trust just anyone to handle that."

"I'll finish my brief on the Scobell case this afternoon. Give me the suggestions. I was a salesman before I was a lawyer." Whitley twisted in the seat and faced Markey. "Look Jud, every executive gets the idea at some time or another that the business can't get along without him. Eventually he dies. If the business folds, it isn't because the one man dies. The reason must go deeper than that. Men are expendable. You've worked like a dog ever since you've been here and if this is to be all work and no fun, is it worth it to anyone that you go jump in an early grave?."

Markey sighed. "Whit, what you're saying has been creeping up on me for a long time. I need a crutch, a sidearm. Someone who can step in and take my place."

"Is it money, the reason why you don't?"

"No. It's the man. I'd say you, but you're tied down to that law."

Whitley grinned and made polishing motions, his nails held against his coat. "Not necessarily."

Markey ogled. "You mean you'd agree to a working vice presidency?"

"Ummm ... well, at a suitable raise in salary, I might. Hell, anyone can look up precedents in a law library."

Markey chuckled and sat back. "Forgive me, boy. I had a notion you wouldn't have it on a platter. As of now you begin. Next board meeting you're installed officially. Now ... by God, I've had that camp in the woods up on Big Bone for three years and I've averaged going once a year. I'm going out there this afternoon and get tanked. See if I don't."

To say that John Sidney Grahame was merely relieved to discover that he hadn't, after all, killed anyone was to be mistaken in his feelings, because he did not allow them to show too much. He was so overjoyed that although tired from a day's work in the woods, he raced over to the school that was only a few hundred yards from his home and caught a kickoff squarely in the face as he ran through the switch canes back of the end zone and out onto the field. For a moment he was stunned ... knocked flat, but he got up shaking his head. He looked toward the group of boys who were laughing at him, saw coach O'Boyle lumbering toward him concernedly only to slow when he saw he wasn't hurt. The kicker had surprised even himself and sent the ball soaring over the head of the receiver. John Sidney laughed. He was feeling too good to be sore. He picked up the ball and casually tossed a sixty yard pass back to the kicker. "Do it again and I'll run it through the pack of you," he said good humoredly.

A chorus of delight went up because none of the boys relished the way he had kicked against them. It came toward him, a little short this time and spinning wildly. "Just my luck to miss it," he said, kicking his shoes off and out of the way, "after making my brags." He didn't miss it however, and instead of racing back upfield, he turned and trotted toward the eastern sidelines. Like a pack of wolves they converged on him and at the very instant of the first impending tackle, he turned like a shot and flashed toward the western sidelines, running like the wind. Four backfield men who had trailed the kick sped to cut him off and two of them, angling in, would have knocked him out of bounds but with a bewildering change of pace, he faked one boy blind then straightened out and simply outran the other one to the goal line.

Boys find it hard to hold grudges and in another second they were around him in an admiring crowd, beating him over the shoulders in good natured camraderie.

O'Boyle, his ulcer acting up, strolled over, glowering savagely. "I hated you after the other day," he growled. "If you ain't gonna come to school, stay the hell away from here and save my reason. Boy, that was a professional run against eleven players without a single man interference.

"He don't need any interference," complained the boy who had been so sharply faked. "He turned plumb around and didn't lose speed."

"No excuses," snapped O'Boyle. "He faked you slap off your feet. How many times I told you don't tackle a man that close to the sidelines. Block him."

"I never got close enough for either one," said the lad frowning. "Say Grahame ... I think that's your name. How come you don't come on and sign up for school?"

John Sidney lost his smile. "Look fellas, I got an uncle to look out for and I got to make a living for both of us. I really didn't come out here to show off. I was just lucky ... and clumsy ... catching one in the chops like I did a while ago. My lips feel a foot thick."

"And," said the boy he had outrun to the goal line, "I feel like Ned in the Primer. I'm first string half back."

While youth sported on the playing field, Judson Markey's jeep wound its slow way up a winding woods road that led six miles through the forest hills and valleys to his camp on Bone River. He could have driven a little farther around and come within half a mile of the camp, but he wouldn't have been able to take the Jeep in as the only road from the highway was a footpath. The back was laden with food. Clucking suggestively, promising lighter spirits was a case of good bonded whiskey.

Markey drove slowly because it fitted his mood. For months he had looked forward to this day. For months he had been telling himself to slow down, but it took Whitley's sharp carping to push him into the act. He had made money for himself and his investors. It was not necessary that he give them his life as well. He had phoned Dr. John Forrest to reassure himself about Hodge's condition, but privately he had to admit that he hadn't been as concerned as a parent should. Whose fault was it? His or his son's, or his wife's? A man did about what he could. Past that fate took over.

Whitley had been right. A hundred years from now the world would little note nor long remember whether in the twentieth century one Judson Ellisade Markey was a success or a failure.

Later he dropped the big steak on the grill and stirred the fire. He dropped a few hickory chips on it to liven the meat with smoke. Plenty of Tabasco too. Esther said it wasn't good for the stomach. His stomach felt fine. To hell with Esther.

CHAPTER FIVE

ohn Sidney went home feeling tired but happy. He was wanted. Actually, he considered going ahead to school, using his college money. He could get through college some way. By the time he faced Uncle Hec across the supper table he had changed his mind again.

As an appetizer Uncle Hec had quaffed a water glass full of gin. In fact, he had had several before he started cooking supper. No matter how drunk he got, Uncle Hec always had a substantial meal ready for John Sidney. Tonight it was a big stew, fragrant and tasty with onions, carrots, celery, potatoes and big tender hunks of beef.

Although they had come south from California, Uncle Hec had been born in the south and one of his boasts was his ability to make cornbread, which he cooked often. Now that he could get stone ground meal they had it almost every day. John Sidney ate heartily and they went into the living room studio to stare at the painting.

Uncle Hec burped delicately. "I took a walk this afternoon," he announced although it was something he usually did every afternoon.

"Oh … See anything?"

"I saw *her* and I read a paper. You didn't kill anyone. I can see why you've been wounded."

"You saw *her*? Yes, I read the paper … *her*?"

"*Her.*" Uncle Hec shifted his bulk in the chair and pointed to the painting. "I was satisfied with her until I saw *her.*" He got up and draped the painting.

"Did she see you?"

"As a matter of fact she did. Since there couldn't be two like her in Taretown, I'd have said none had I been asked, I assumed she must be Delani. Peculiar sort of name. So I asked her."

John Sidney felt a cold chill in his stomach. "You asked her?"

"I asked her. She stopped and looked at me. I can still feel it. Like diving into clear blue water. She looked at me for a moment, then said, 'Yes sir. I'm Delani.' Then I had to have my joke. I said, 'I'm your Uncle Hec.' She didn't know just how to take it for a moment, so I added, 'I'm John Sidney's Uncle Hec.' She got it then and if I could just catch the exact shade of her blush with my brush I could die happy. I never saw anything like it ... and her body." Uncle Hec shook his head. "It's bad for a man my age to see something like that. It's demoralizing. Still unenriched by the delirium of love, still lacking the last touch of maturity, but all the more exciting for it. She's a tender, half opened bud ... not the full blown rose as yet."

"What else did she say," asked John Sidney impatiently.

"Well, she managed a smile. Seemed like she wanted to run again. She said, 'Tell him ... '" Uncle Hec stopped and felt for the gin bottle.

"Tell him what?" insisted John Sidney, sitting on the edge of the chair.

"It never quite came out. She blushed again and turned and ran. She ran like a deer, lightly, with a stride as graceful as a fairy ... which is the way a fairy should run."

John Sidney relaxed, a bitter taste in the back of his throat.

"*Good evening.*" The brassy echoes of a strident voice shook the loose panes throughout the living room, and they both turned toward the open front door in which stood a formidible female.

"Well, dammit, don't I get invited in?" She strode across the threshold without waiting to be asked and stood in the center of the room.

"Er, of course," said Uncle Hec, getting to his feet. "You startled us a bit, that's all."

"Well," she barked, "I'm Miss Martha Wyntringham. I live out Crayville way, but I got interests here in Taretown."

"Please sit down, Miss Martha," said John Sidney, in something of a fog. Miss Martha seemed to think everyone should know her.

"It's about time … and I suppose that old sot of an uncle will insist on hogging the gin."

Uncle Hec blushed violently, something John Sidney had never seen him do, the newness of it, making him giggle. Uncle Hec glared at him and said, "Get Miss Martha a glass and some …"

"Never mind the fluff and flapdoodle. The bottle's got a mouth, ain't it?"

She took the bottle, swigged thirstily and handed it back. "*Growfph*," she said, approximately. "That was what I needed for the job." She stretched thick muscular legs in front of her, rummaged in a purse the size of a small gladstone and extracted a package of cigarettes. "Have one, Hec," she said thrusting the package at him. "John Sid here ain't got the habit, unless I been wrong informed."

John Sidney looked at her carefully. She was just a shade under six feet tall and must have weighed close to two hundred pounds.

"Now," she said when she had her six inch long brown cigarette going, "As I said, I'm Miss Martha. But … you're new here and don't know me. Some people call me 'The Empress' just to impress me. I'm impressed … just as far as I want to be. I got money, I got land, I got power. I can make certain people jump through hoops. I like football. I like Mike O'Boyle. That's the only reason why he stayed here." She flicked her eyes to John Sidney. "Mike O'Boyle says you're the sweetest runner, passer, kicker since … oh he mentioned a dozen or so All-Americans. I forget who all. Says you got to work to buy gin for this old four flusher of an uncle. I say it's a goddamned shame, so I came to offer to keep the old rip soaked in it for free, if that's what it takes. We want you, boy. We want you on the team.

Uncle Hec just gasped and John Sidney felt as though he had been knocked down by a high wind.

"Mrs. Martha Wyntringham. Been married three times. Wish I had all three right now, but dammit they went and died on me. I guess I was too much for 'em. People still call me 'Miss Martha.' That's the south for you. Y'all yankees?"

"Well, we come from California …" Uncle Hec began, but she cut him off.

"Yankees," she dropped it like a bomb. "No … not really. Yankees'll do in a pinch, but Californians …" She made an impolite noise with her mouth. "Everything out there is synthetic, even their grass. Can't grow it. Also a lot of synthetic men and women out there." She looked at them sharply. "I always say, start the worms walkin' and the apples will run if they can. Been here long?"

"About a month," said Uncle Hec carefully.

She swiveled her head to John Sidney. "Son, I talk too much and blow when I'm not talkin'. We'd like to have you at school."

John Sidney shook his head. "I'm sorry Miss Martha. I'd like to but … well, not this year. Maybe next."

"Not good enough. What's your objection to a little help?"

"That'd be subsidizing an athlete."

She nodded slowly. "Yeah … and it'd be the first time too. What other objection you got?"

Uncle Hec rose to the occasion. "We appreciate what you offer Mrs. Wyntringham …"

"Miss Martha," she snapped.

"Miss Martha. I've never encouraged the boy to accept charity."

Miss Martha was silent for a moment. "Ah … so that's it. Who offered you charity?"

There was a long silence.

"We never got around to an offer," she pounded on. "What I offer is this. A loan to carry the boy through school and to keep you in gin. He'll use his own money to go to college, which will be duck soup, because he'll be hounded by every college from Florida to Oregon to attend their school and play football. I like Louisiana State. If he'll go there, I'll make it worth his while. A loan … repayable every cent of it at four percent interest. A legal note made out. The one provision left out will be a time limit. I won't push the boy."

Uncle Hec was calmer now. His eyes met hers and held. "I'd like to know two things. One, why haven't you wanted to know why I don't work. Two, how do you know so much about us?"

"I know about you because I took the trouble to find out. As for the second … the first rather!" She was silent for a while and the belligerence went out of her eyes. "Hector, I guess I figured enough people had already asked you that."

His lips twitched for a moment, then abruptly and walked out of the room muttering something about getting another bottle of gin.

John Sidney felt a tremendous wave of affection for Miss Martha sweep over him. How exquisitely sensitive she was. Her answer was the only one that in kindness she could have made.

His throat was thick and he cleared it. "That was a beautiful thing you said, Miss Martha. He'll love you forever for it."

"Why *doesn't* he work son? He looks as strong as an ox."

"He's an artist. He doesn't know how to do anything. He can't even mow grass effectually. It always looked gaped and butchered. My father always looked out after him. Since my father's death, I've looked out after him … and he after me. I know him so much better than I did my father. My father, acording to Uncle Hec, was always looking for 'way out yonder,' a Beowolf searching for a Grendel … a Galahad searching for the Grail that was not to be found, only hunted. He was an air ace in two wars. He was killed in Korea."

Miss Martha said, "You say he paints? Hector, I mean?"

"Yes, but he paints beauty as he sees it, and I must say as I see it too. I like to think that Uncle Hec paints beauty as it is. They've called him a calendar artist, a draftsman, but he's no draftsman. There's too much life and laughter and emotion in his works."

"Is that one of his?"

"Yes ma'm."

"Could I see it?"

"I'd rather he'd show you. I think he will."

Uncle Hec came back with a fifth of gin. "Have a snort, Miss Martha" he said, recovered now.

She took a hefty one, cleared her throat and lit another of her expensive imported cigarettes. "Hector, the boy tells me you're an artist."

"He and I think so," said Uncle Hec shortly.

"I have an open mind. May I see the one you have draped there?"

"It isn't finished."

"*Uncle Hec*" said John Sidney, so sharply that the older man jumped.

He grinned. "All right. I'm a little sensitive about my stuff because there's always something wrong with it that I can never see. I will *not* paint a monstrosity, I will *not* paint something morbid, dreary or unhappy. Maybe that's where I'm wrong."

"If you're wrong, then the world of art has gone to hell on a one wheeled bicycle" she snapped, "and I have a lot of evidence that it has. Let's see the work."

He undraped the painting and stood back.

Miss Martha stared at it for a good five minutes, examining it minutely. She took out another cigarette and lit it. "You want to know what's wrong with the painting?"

"I do" he said seriously.

She shrugged. "Nothing. It is perfectly wonderful piece of work ... marvelous. It's colors are a delight to the eyes, its impression of depth is astonishing. Painting went to hell when cameras came into being. The reason being that there were so few *good* artists. For my money an artist that paints a moon hanging over a barn to look like a piece of maggoty cheese hanging over a blob of warm manure is simply a poor artist. The son of a bitch couldn't paint a recognizable canvas if his life depended upon it so what he does paint must be *explained*. I can show you the same thing in poetry. Anything worth looking at can either be identified or at least some sort of emotional response derived. Anything written in English that can't be understood is just damn poor writing and I don't give a hootnanny-what. That is just as true of poetry, as prose, as art, as the direction on a road sign. Did you ever show your stuff?"

Uncle Hec sat down. He had not been prepared for such a broadside and he was somewhat weakened by the vehemence of it. "Yes, I've had shows. I've even sold four canvasses. Why do you ask?"

"Oh, no particular reason. Maybe I will have a particular reason later. Right now I'd like to know if I can lend the boy, or you, some money. Last but not least, I want this painting."

There was silence. Miss Martha reddened and snorted. "I know what you're thinking. I buy the painting so as make the deal work. That's a lie, and if you don't know when someone honestly likes your work, then no damn wonder you don't know what's wrong with it ... and are always thinking something *is* because some jerk critic gave you the back of his hand Where is he now and what has he ever done?" She eyed them for a moment, then with an angry incoherent explosion she turned and marched to the door. "Write me a goddamned letter." She turned and disappeared.

Uncle Hec stared at the door for a long moment, then cleared his throat. "Son ..."

"I know" said John Sidney, staring at the floor. "I don't know just what we did, but it was wrong."

"How true. She *did* like the painting. She did want to buy it."

"Yes, she did. We sat here and let her believe things that aren't true. We'll have to put it right."

"Something else" said Uncle Hec with a peculiar timbre in his voice. "I'm about to give an order."

John Sidney smiled. Uncle Hec had given precious few orders since he could remember. "What's that?"

"We accept Miss Martha's offer. You go to school."

John Sidney nodded slowly. "Yes, I think so. I think I felt that way before you gave the order."

"I surmised as much. I guess that's why I gave it.

"Something about that woman" said Uncle Hec shaking his head thoughtfully. "I'm switched if she didn't fill this room up. Talk about personalities …"

"She certainly is one. I'll tell Mr. Slocum tomorrow that I'm quitting. I have a boundary line to blaze for him. I'll do that before I quit. I'll tell Coach O'Boyle …"

"You might tell *her* too. I think she'd want to know."

"Yes … What made you think of that?"

"Oh, I don't know. It just occurred to me."

"It appears that you don't object to her. Being a Negro, I mean."

"I doubt seriously that any man could object to her if he had any appreciation for the finer things. His prejudices might obscure his vision, but I never could foster a prejudice that threatened my reason."

"Don't most of them?"

"They all do. Will you write Miss Martha?"

"I'll do better than that. I'll go see her."

"How?"

"On my feet. I need the conditioning."

CHAPTER SIX

J udson Markey felt fine. He'd had a good night's sleep and he
waked clear eyed and refreshed.

There were a lot of chores to do.

Two hours later he sat down at a rustic table made of wooden
slabs and smelled the aroma of the fish as they lay before him
on a big platter. The potatoes, their hides black and crisp but the
insides white and mealy, steaming and fragrant and running yel-
low with butter, were beside the platter. French bread and a tall
cool bottle of Liebfraumilch completed the spread. The fish had
that rare elegance that one finds only when it is taken from the
water, cleaned and cooked before it stops wiggling. It had a pun-
gent smoky bite and the sauce provided a tongue tickling tingle.

Carla Smith, foster sister of Delani Smith, daughter of
Mamma Dell Smith drove her modest sedan along at a speed that
was no barometer of her feelings. She drove at a sedate forty-five
miles an hour, but her mind seethed with resentment. To begin
with she heartily disliked Mr. Carlton, the principal who seemed
to think she owed him tribute for the privilege of teaching in his
school. Secondly, he had saddled upon her a job that fell normally
to the coach, that of depositing Fridays football gate receipts in
the Taretown bank. The coach was laid up with a sprained ankle,
so out of twenty possibles, the principal had chosen her. She had
deposited the money, endured the sly lecherous glances of the
man who waited on her and was headed back to school.

The school taught a great deal of agriculture and was built on a large tract of land which the students used in their school work. It was ten miles from Taretown, centrally located so it would be of easier access to the children of the county.

Mr. Carlton was something of a tyrant and a rider of privilege, but so far she had escaped the object of his attention. He was a married man and Carla used it as her defense although her dislike was a great deal more fundamental.

Her car sputtered again. She looked at the fuel gauge and saw with dismay that it registered empty. Gas thieves again, she thought, her jaws tight with rage. It was the second time in a month they had drained her tank. She pulled off to the side of the gravelled road and got out, listening. Not a car did she hear or see. She glanced at her watch and saw that she had a class in fifteen minutes. Missing the class would be a minor thing, but the thought of having to explain running out of gas to the sarcastic Mr. Carlton was a fearful annoyance.

To the east across a deep wooded ravine she saw a house nestled among the trees ... a camp, as she knew, having passed the place many times. She thought she could see the squatty outlines of a jeep. Maybe the owner was in residence. Maybe he'd sell her some gas.

She crossed the road, discovered a path and followed it windingly down into the ravine and climbed out on the other side. The sun was hot and Carla dabbed a deposit of sweat from her upper lip and forehead. She stood looking from a height down on the camp. She could see a man eating in front of the place. She smoothed her light blue orlon dress to fit the rich swells of her hips and started down the incline toward the camp. She walked with a free lithe stride that was as graceful as a dance. She was tall and strongly built, her legs softly rounded but threaded with powerful muscle, her waist small, her stomach flat and hard and her breasts magnificent promontories, erect and firm.

"Good afternoon, sir."

Judson Markey started and looked around. "Oh … Hello. You startled me for a moment." He did a double take and looked again, Carla noting the act and cursing the traitorous flush that mantled her cheeks. It was a very becoming blush and he laughed. "Sorry if I stared. You see, my mind was a million miles away and seeing a naiad in cream-bronze step out the mists of my mind … unasked as it were, was startling. What can I do for you?"

Her respiration, accelerated by the frank admiration in his eyes, the utter honesty of his reaction and the smooth caress of his complimentary speech, now began to slow down. "I … I ran out of gas over on the road, sir. If you have any to spare I'd be glad to buy enough to get me back to school. I teach and I'm already late for my class."

He shook his head and shoveled fish into his mouth. "Sorry. I don't have any gas." He brightened. "But there's some in the jeep. Tell you what. Since you're already late, what say you let me finish eating and I'll siphon some out. The taste of gas might spoil my fish."

"You're very kind" she said softly, so much so that his eyes flicked up at her and she cursed the impulse that had toned her voice down and made it satiny. "I wouldn't allow you to spoil your meal. If you have a hose I'll siphon it myself … and if you have a container." She smiled revealing her even white teeth. "I don't seem to have anything but a hungry car."

"Nope. I insist on being hospitable and while I'm at it, come sit with me and eat some of this delicious fish and a baked potato. There's beer and Liebfraumilch.

Refusal was on her lips but again she was betrayed by an impulse. "It does look and smell delicious. If you'll fix me a plate,

I'll sit here on the steps and eat." She smiled making twin dimples dig deep into her cheeks. "I'm really quite hungry, like my car. I missed my lunch."

"I'm Judson Markey" he said quietly, "I'm white by no more choice than you're not. Please sit with me and eat all you want." His face lost its serious look as he smiled. "I'm even hoping you're not in too big a hurry."

Her heart took a leap that threatened to stagger her, but she survived the moment and sat down shyly. "I don't think I ever did this before" she said, a catch in her voice.

His eyes came up, serious again. "You mean sitting with a white person?"

"Yes sir, and like you said, I've already missed the class."

"We're about to eat together and we've never been introduced. I'm Judson Markey." He extended a big hand.

She smiled nervously. "I'm Carla Smith." Her own slender fingers closed around his hand and for a moment it seemed that a licking bolt of electricity travelled between them. They both felt it, both knew it and it was a sobering thing. She disengaged her hand slowly, her full red lips parted and her breasts as they lifted and fell were some measure of her perturbation. His eyes held hers for a brief moment. His amber and steady, hers a soft flower-heart brown, also steady.

"Here, let me help your plate." He loaded it with fish and placed a big split and buttered potato on it. "That's good French bread. Tear it as you want it. I never like to cut good bread."

Carla was hungry, and the fish excellent, but she ate with difficulty. The touch of this man she had never seen before had shaken her terribly. That he was not an ordinary man had been obvious from the moment he spoke. Carla Smith well knew the difference between good people and trash. The line had been vividly drawn for her by Mamma Dell long ago. She knew a great many white people who respected her mind and her person, who spoke to her on a single level without patronization. So had the man seated before her, but there was a difference. She had attracted him. He had said so freely, without the slightest flicker of hesitation. Carla was too much of a woman not to know when she attracted a man. She had attracted many. The tiny potent bolt of lightning that attended the touch of their hands had reached him as well as her. This she knew.

When it happened, it was so shocking and sudden that she was frozen into immobility. One moment he was eating, the next he was a stricken man on his feet, his mouth wide and his eyes staring. He caught the table with both hands and made a bubbly croaking noise. He pointed to his throat and reeled, back, falling heavily to the ground. She screamed, harshly, tearingly, still shocked out of action, not knowing what to do, knowing that she was watching a man die. She screamed a second time so shrilly that John Sidney's nerves prickled from the sharpness of it. He dropped his blazing-axe and raced to her side. "What happened?"

"He swallowed a fish bone … I think … He's dying … Oh God … he's *dying …*"

It raced through his mind like the slice of a razor … the story of a corpsman during the war who did an emergency operation on a man's throat in time to save his life. He inserted the barrel of a fountain pen … A cane, that would have to do. With frantic haste he cut a joint from a nearby fishing pole and knelt by Markey whose face was growing purple.

"Hold this'" he said sharply, handing her the joint of cane. He felt the man's throat, selected a space between two rings of tracheal cartilage and made a single sure slice. His knife, as always, was razor sharp and the wound stood open redly. He made another cut, getting between the cartilages, then snatching the cane worked it carefully into the opening. Breath whistled through the makeshift tube and a shudder of relief passed over the stricken man. Gradually he lost the horrible plum color ... it faded to bluish then the pasty dirty white of a stricken person. Finally his opened flutteringly.

"Go get a sheet from inside" said John Sidney crisply. "Tear me some two inch strips. We'll have to bind this for the trip to town ... which is the nearest way?"

"Over there" she pointed, toward her own car across the ravine. "I think this road leads to the gravelled road. This other way is too long ... through the woods. This way it's a mile to the blacktop and about four from here to town." She ran to get the sheet, tearing it frantically on her way back. With swift sure hands John Sidney wound the strips around Markey's throat, securing the tube well.

"Now, if you'll help me get him to the jeep." They got Markey into the jeep but he was still in bad shape, his body still jerking from anoxia and shock.

"You're going to have to ride with him in the back" said John Sidney with an accurate evaluation of conditions.

She nodded and got in. She sat far to one side and John Sidney gently let Markey back until his head was in her lap. He arranged the man's long legs as comfortably as possible then got in the jeep, started the motor and scooted off through the woods toward the road.

To call the tidal wave of activity that struck the Taretown Clinic a disturbance would leave the condition half described. Markey was swept from the jeep on a stretcher and Dr. Forrest summoned frantically. A nurse's aide feeling like Paul Revere phoned the plant and poured out a partly coherent, generally inaccurate account of what had happened.

Whitley, the attorney, and greater and lesser lights from plant management converged upon the clinic in a cloud. In the midst of all the activity John Sidney and Carla faded out and by common consent met at the jeep.

"You're Delani's sister, aren't you?" he said, his eyes regarding her with somber interest.

"Yes …" Her own eyes widened perceptably. "Oh … you're Mr. Grahame. You live across the ravine from us."

"That's right. I'm John Sidney Grahame."

She clasped her slender fingers nervously. "I suppose you're wondering why I was at the camp?"

He nodded. "It went through my mind."

She licked her lips and gripped her hands tighter. "It isn't what you think. I …"

He smiled slowly. "I haven't had a thought on the matter, one way or another. There wasn't time. I said it went through my mind such as what anyone was doing there." The smile faded. "And another thing, what either of you were doing there is very much no business of mine."

She flushed and the tide of pink surging up beneath the creamy bronze of her skin made her beauty lash out at him. "I just didn't want you to think …"

"I haven't thought" he reminded her gently. "Would you like to tell me why you were there?" He could see that she did want to explain but her efforts were stumbling and embarrassing to her.

"I ran out of gas … we went by my car on the way out. I'd gone over there to ask him for some. He was in the middle of his meal and he very kindly invited me to join him." She reddened again. "I was so hungry that I did. We were eating when he started choking. I screamed …"

"You surely did" he agreed with a grin. "A voice like yours could peel the bark from a tree. I was coming at a dead run before I had any idea what had happened."

She shivered. "Mr. Grahame ... I"m so glad you came. I'm so glad it was you. I don't think I ever saw anything done so smoothly. You seemed to know exactly what you were doing."

He lowered his eyes a trifle. "I read a story about it. I was impressed because it was something it seemed a good idea to know. I even discussed it with a doctor once."

She sighed. "Well, I suppose we've done what we can here I am five miles from my car and still no gas. I suppose at school they think I've had a wreck."

"I think we've earned some privileges. I'll run you back in the jeep."

She was almost tearfully grateful. "Would you? I just don't know how I'd get back there if you didn't. It'd take some time and I'm probably in dutch as it is."

CHAPTER SEVEN

John Sidney took Carla to her car then drove back to town, got directions to the Markey home, and parked the jeep around behind the house out of the way of the drive so that the other cars might come and go without intereference. As he got out he looked toward the smooth modern house and saw someone standing near the back door, just outside it.

She was young, lovely and just bursting into exciting nubility, her curves poetically extravagant, and she conscious of every one of them. He could feel it, he could see it in the way she carried her body, like a conscious flaunting of it, throwing it wholly toward anything male. Like a flower bending toward a neighbor or following the sun. He had the chilling conviction that in the nude he would not be able to find a single wrinkle in her fabulous skin, so fully charged was it with healthy young flesh.

The vision smiled and walked toward him. "Hi" she said. "You're John Sidney Grahame."

"Yes ... how did you know?"

"I was watching football practice the other day when you ran through the whole team by yourself. You were wonderful."

"Thanks" he said drily. "Any word from your father."

"None ... other than that they're operating. Where did you get the jeep?"

He told her in crisp frugal sentences what had happened. He left Carla out of it in deference to what he supposed her desires to be.

Patti's eyes grew large and she came quite close ... too close. "Then you're the one who brought him in. You saved his life."

"That can get tiresome" he told her shortly.

She withdrew, a little hurt. "You shouldn't resent an honest compliment ... it's the truth. You did save his life. Won't you come in and have a ... drink or something?"

"No, thank you," he said and turning, walked off leaving her quivering with a vague punishing resentment.

He went straight home, his breast in a turmoil that now had two main ingredients.

Delani whom nothing could erase, and a new quantity, that of the disturbing Patti Markey. She'd been dressed in a black knit creation that could have been an exotic gym suit or a swim suit that was not intended to get wet. He felt certain that beneath it had been nothing. He was not insensitive to the invitation that had gone unspoken. Neither was he moved by it.

There was a car standing before the house and a tall muscular young man who seemed thin, as from an illness. Uncle Hec and the stranger sat on the porch and watched him come up the walk.

"John Sidney, allow me to present Mr. Norman McLeod. He's a reporter."

John Sidney's heart sank but he instinctively liked the sardonic faced man. They shook hands.

"I've been to the hospital," said McLeod without preamble. "I got such a jambalaya of nonsense that I'm trying to get the story. After assiduous nosing about I find you're the one who brought him in. Want to tell me about it?"

John Sidney nodded. "I brought him in."

McLeod looked at Uncle Hec. "Talkative, ain't he?"

"I talk too much" said Uncle Hec with a grin. "He doesn't talk enough. We are a family of extremes."

McLeod studied the serious eyes. "It'll come out some day when Mr. Markey can talk. Right now there's all sorts of nonsense that might get to the papers. If I can have an eyewitness account, then at least the truth will be printed."

It made sense to John Sidney, so he told the story again.

McLeod who used his memory rather than a notebook and nodded. "Well, that makes sense. Now, about this colored girl that helped you. Tell me more about her."

"Her name is Carla Smith. She teaches school."

"What was she doing at his camp?"

"I didn't consider it any of my business, so I didn't ask her."

McLeod grinned. "Son, I've been shot at by everything that can throw a missile. I don't wound easy. If I can get the story from you, I won't have to bother her."

John Sidney pondered for a moment. "It's nothing to be ashamed of. She ran out of gas and went to the camp to borrow some."

"Why didn't you want to tell me?"

The steady eyes came up and McLeod was annoyed that they disconcerted him. "I don't pry. I don't like prying people. I'll tell you this much. There was more to it than borrowing gas, although that was the number one reason. Just what else is not necessary to your story, and it isn't my place to tell you. Neither will she tell you."

McLeod said nothing and looked toward the high school. He was an intelligent man. He didn't push his luck. Also he rather thought he had uncovered something that might be a private matter, and as John Sidney pointed out, not a part of the story he wanted.

"Dr. Forrest did say that you did a very creditable emergency tracheotomy. If you hadn't they'd have had to bury Markey.

Forrest said he couldn't have lived more than a few minutes longer."

"I'm glad he's all right. Did they get the fishbone out?"

"Yes. The doctor said he must have been really gobbling that fish to let a bone that size get in his throat and cause a spasm that would have choked him to death."

"Is it necessary to bring her into the story?"

"Would it be complete without her?"

John Sidney shrugged. "I guess not."

"Son, if you're worried about my treatment of the story, let me assure you that even newsmen have ethics. As you say, any other color that crept into the picture is not a part of the story. There won't be any mention of anything but what is news."

"Thank you." John Sidney then told him the story in detail.

McLeod nodded when he finished. "See, her part will be just as you've told me. Why didn't you just keep quiet about the other? The hinting that she discovered something that she hadn't anticipated."

John Sidney shook his head. "Mr. McLeod, this had been a pretty full day."

"Yes, I can see that, but you don't have to worry. By the way, I spoke to a Miss Lynn Anne Jones yesterday … about her ordeal the other night. To prove my point about what I write and what I choose not to, I'm leaving it so it appears that some girl broke young Markey's neck."

John Sidney went stiff and his eyes narrowed. "Why did you choose her, and what did she have to do with it?"

"Nothing probably. I just had an impulse to talk to her … there was an opportunity and I took it. I just wanted to talk to her about the problems she might have run into with the sons of the management of the Plant."

John Sidney looked at the sweat glistening in his palms for a long moment. "Did she talk for publication?"

"No. It won't be published. You see, I was following down an idea I have … that a sort of dank stinking fear rides this town. A lot of poor men went to work at the Plant. They never had it so good. They've been poor so long they can't believe their good luck. They're not quite rational about anything that might appear as a threat to their jobs."

"This business about sons of management," put in Uncle Hec. "You're working on the idea that with daughters of the men who have jobs, the boys might be taking unfair advantage?"

"Something like that. I can report a happy circumstance though. Management and upper echelon worker men who might just be able to throw their weight around if they chose have between them eight teen-age boys. There are only two who might fit my idea. One is out of circulation with a badly used neck. The other one is still operating but there's nothing I can pin on him yet."

John Sidney looked up. "You say talking to Lynn Anne Jones was just coincidence?"

"Yes. Why?"

John Sidney shook his head. "Just looks like there are too many coincidences happening around for comfort." He didn't elaborate and McLeod didn't press the matter. He stood up to leave and offered a hand to John Sidney, who took it.

"Lynn Anne is a fine lovely little girl" he said softly. "The kind that goes in for hero worship."

When he had gone John Sidney ran a hand over his face. It was still damp. "I guess she told him."

"I'm sure she did" said Uncle Hec. "Just the same, I -don't think anything she told him will ever get into print."

"The arm of coincidence gets longer every day."

"I meant to ask you what you meant by that."

John Sidney took a trembling breath. "I'm there when Markey tries to rape Lynn Anne. I'm maybe fifty yards away, carefully blazing out a skidder line for Mr. Slocum when I hear Carla's scream. I'm not thinking about anything much except school and Delani, and Miss Martha and your painting ..."

"Nothing much" said Uncle Hec with a grin.

"That's right, then right out of a clear sky this scream ... like a jagged glass ... something you could shave with and there I am."

"Twice in a week" said Uncle Hec. "That's not too bad."

"I decide to walk in the ravine last night and there's Delani who also decided to walk in the ravine at the same time. Today it's Carla, Delani's foster sister who screams and there I am."

John Sidney stood up. "I think I'll go tell Delani about my plans."

The sun was lowering in the west in a bath of boiling fire. So rampant were the colors that John Sidney paused and looked at them for a while. It seemed that such color should have sound.

"Good evening" she said and John Sidney wasn't in the least surprised. It seemed perfectly natural even though he had expected to find her on her side of the ravine.

"Hello. I was just ..."

"And I beat you to it" she said. Her lips parted in a smile and her teeth glistened. "I'm a very bold woman."

John Sidney chuckled. "Then you admit you were looking for me."

There was no embarrassment, no denial in her eyes. "I've been looking for you. I saw you step off the back porch."

Uncle Hec stepped out on the porch and waved to them. "Delani, I'm a topping cook and I have left-over stew, collards, hot cornbread, green onions and buttermilk for supper. Care to join us?"

John Sidney could see the tightening of her diaphragm as emotion struck her. I'd love to sir ... if.

"He asked you" put in John Sidney quietly. "Now I'm asking you."

"But ..."

"He asked you. I asked you. I know what you're thinking. We still ask you."

Her olive tanned skin turned a dusky pink. "Please ... don't misunderstand me. There's nothing I'd like better, but I don't want to cause any trouble ... people to talk ..."

"We both ask you" he insisted gently.

"May I run ask Mamma Dell?"

"Yes."

She turned and walked away, her lithe sumptuously curved body swaying with such delicate grace that John Sidney's eyes stung. He could see the tininess of her waist, the cleft in her back, the smooth flicker of conditioned muscle that flashed as she walked. The motion of her rounded hips was the sheerest poetry ... the shadows of the ravine swallowed her up.

"And now" said Uncle Hec gustily, "let's take a good deep breath. We're not hibernating amphibians."

John Sidney turned and looked at his uncle. "Thanks" he said strangely.

"For what?"

"For your approval. It means a lot to know that someone realizes, knows, and approves."

Uncle Hec sighed again. "I see, I know, I realize ... and I approve. The approval comes from inside without notice to outside considerations. Once in a while one appears, like her. Not very often boy. One appeared to me once. Something like her with the face of an angel and the mind of a sewer. It probably won't happen to you because false flowers don't grow wild. You have the advantage of seeing her in the natural state, so to speak. I saw mine a lacquered over with civilized camouflage and I couldn't pierce it."

"Do you suppose she'll come?"

"I rather think she will. Mamma Dell will decide, I suppose."

Mamma Dell examined the face of the girl more to gain time than to see anything. This was a moment she had been dreading for many a year and now that it was here, she couldn't see that the years had helped in preparing her for what she had to say.

"So they asked you to supper?"

"Yes'm. What do you think I ought to do?"

Mamma Dell looked at her quietly for a moment. "What do you want to do—"?

"I want to go."

Mamma Dell nodded her head and sighed. "Yes, I recon you do."

Her indecision was manifest, so Delani asked the dreaded question. "Mamma Dell, who am I?"

"Honey, I know you got a right to know. Right this minute I can't answer you. To begin with, it ain't in my hands alone. I ain't kep' this secret all these years 'cause I liked to. You just set here for a minnit. I'll be back." She got up with astounding agility remembering her years and went into Carla's room. Carla lay on her bed in pants and bra, one satin skinned arm thrown over her, across her face. She seemed asleep, but her mind was working furiously.

"Baby, you sleep?" asked Mamma Dell softly.

Carla removed her arm. "No'm. You wanted something?"

Mamma Dell sighed gustily and sat down. "Well, it's here. All these years I been shakin' my head over that gal and now its come. Seems like Mr. Grahame … Mr. Hector and that boy, they asked her to eat supper with 'em. She come to ask me if it was all right. God knows there ain't nuthin' wrong with her eatin' with them people, but … you know where we live."

Carla sat up and slid to the side of the bed, her magnificent body glowing softly in the dim light. "Mamma Dell, let her go."

Mamma Dell nodded slowly. "You shot that right at me. You didn't think it over. That ain't like you. But … since you come home this evening, there ain't been anything like you. You'll tell me, I 'spect, but you'll take your own time doin' it."

"Yes'm. I'll tell you someday. Let her go."

"But you don't know neither one of them."

"Yes, I know the boy. He's a fine gentleman."

"No longer'n two days ago you was wonderin' about them people, right along with the rest of us."

"Yes'm. That was two days ago. I know now. I'll tell you about it."

Mamma Dell got up and walked back to her own room. She could sense the tautness of the girl as she watched her. She nodded, "I reckon it's all right this time … but don't you think you oughta put on some different clothes?"

"Could I wear my party dress?"

" 'Course you can, but don't spill nuthin on it. It's the only one you got."

"Can I ask him over, some time?"

Mamma Dell took some time to think this over. "Well … I reckon it wouldn't be very nice not to, not after he asked you to supper."

Delani leaped forward, embraced the old woman and kissed her noisily on the cheek. "Thank you, Mamma Dell. I know you didn't agree to this without some thinking."

Mamma Dell shook her head. "I just hope to God I'm doin' the right thing. I don't know. I just don't know."

Her hair had been drawn back tightly and confined by a circlet of gold colored metal. It fanned out richly at the nape of her neck, the effect being to expose her face and reveal its almost Grecian purity. Her party dress was strapless, of some weighty lavender cotton material and exquisitely laundered. It was last year's dress and Delani was a growing girl. The resultant fit and the patrician air with which she wore it struck John Sidney speechless.

He just stood and looked at her until a wave of blood rising to her cheeks brought him back to reality.

"I'm sorry," he said, dropping his eyes. "I'm sorry and yet I'm not. You're so beautiful that I can't believe it."

She caught her breath. Tears sprang into her eyes, intensifying the hurtful longing that threatened to stifle him.

"Did I say something ..." He stepped from the porch and took her by the arm.

"No, no ...", she laughed shakily. "It's just that ..." She shook her head. "I just came eighteen and no one ever told me such a thing before. I guess it shook me up."

"Come on in," he said, assisting her up the steps. "Let's say we shook each other up. You did it first. Uncle Hec, look here."

Uncle Hec closed the door of the oven and stood up. For an eternity, it seemed to her, he looked and again she blushed selfconsciously. Uncle Hec shook his head. "I'm too old to be subjected to any such vision," he complained. "Just for that, I'm going to take a drink of gin." Shaking his head he took the bottle from the sideboard and took a long swig. "You two go on into the living room. Supper'll be ready in a jiffy." Angrily he swallowed the lump in his throat. Beauty always did that to Hector Grahame. This child was something that made chills race over his spine, a child-woman, so exquisitely chiseled that in his entire life he had never seen anyone who could match her yet he knew this was not true.

For Uncle Hec and John Sidney supper was a spasm of time during which they went through the motions of eating. Delani ate with a healthy appetite and full appreciation of Uncle Hec's culinary talents.

Later when she and John Sidney stood in the back yard in the gathering darkness, time resumed its normal beat for the boy. "I'm going back to school" he said.

"I'm so glad." She was glad. It was something he could feel, like he could shut his eyes and feel her presence. It was something fluffy-pink, evanescent and tinted ever so faintly with a kind of perfume that seemed to be herself, rather than artifice. Her eyes were too steady for him and he looked aside.

"Will you play football?"

He looked up. "How did you know I play?"

"I watched you the other day, the day you ran that kick back. You were so sure on your feet, so balanced and always in command of yourself."

He felt less so at the moment, listening to her naked admiration. "Thanks" he muttered.

"I wish I could see you play."

"Can't you?"

"I mean …" She laughed a little ruefully. "Am I being an upstart to want to watch you from the stands like anyone else?"

"No. I don't think you could be an upstart, if you wanted to."

She touched his hand It was just a simple friendly contact, but it raged through his nervous system like high voltage. "That was a very nice think to say."

"I guess I couldn't have helped myself. It was like I was listening to someone else speak."

Her teeth gleamed as she chuckled. "Maybe it came from the heart."

"It did ... all the way. I don't think I've ever spoken a word to you that didn't. I don't think I could."

The faint illumination that came to them from the stars and distant street lamps revealed that he had touched her. Her eyes swam in a crystal bath and the action of her breasts advertised the increase in respiration. She bit her lips, seemingly to keep back some exquisitely wonderful rush of emotion.

As before at their first meeting, John Sidney felt a wild desire to do something, anything to asage the tumult in his chest. He could scarcely believe that she could do such a thing to him, but she did, every time he saw her. She was so sensitive as was he to everything, every little word every nuance, that passed between them. That he loved her did not now have the slightest chance of denying. It was something that he knew like he knew the sun would rise tomorrow. He sensed that she felt the same way about him, but he was not schooled enough in the game of life to know what to do next. He was too long about it, too overwhelmed to act and the moment passed. He felt like screaming, doing foolish things to relieve the the moment. She gave a fluttery sigh. "I enjoyed the supper. Thank you and your uncle so much." She turned and the night swallowed her up.

John Sidney went back into the house weakened by emotion, a dry bitterness in his mouth from the lost opportunity. He could have kissed her. He knew it well, but he had let the opportunity go by while he stood there tongue tied and helpless.

The next day he registered, but told Coach O'Boyle, "I won't be out for practice this afternoon. I have some unfinished business to attend to."

CHAPTER EIGHT

J ohn Sidney took the old road to avoid traffic toward where
he'd been told Miss Martha Wyntringham lived, and started
out at a fast dogtrot. For a good mile he held it then dropped into
a relaxed walk for a few hundred yards, then began his trot again.
At this rate the eight miles didn't seem too long, but his clothes
were dank with sweat when at last he came to a spot where he
could see the magnificent old mansion perched atop the long hill
surrounded by age old trees; oak, beech, pine and magnolia. It
was still a long walk but he made it sedately without running and
finally knocked at the double front doors beneath a tremendous
fanlight of stained glass.

A light coffee-colored maid with an outrageously voluptuous
figure, smouldering sultry eyes and deep dimples like Carla
Smith answered the door. "Yes sir?"

"I'd like to see Miss Martha, if you please."

"Yes sir. Won't you some in?"

"Thank you."

She ushered him into a tremendous parlor with floor to ceiling
mirrors, a huge fireplace filled with oak logs ready to light, crowned
by an ornate marble mantel and another tall slim mirror with a gilt
frame. There were family portraits on the light blue plastered walls,
and the windows were draped with heavy royal blue velvet.

"Please have a seat, sir, and I'll tell Miss Martha you're here."
The maid smiled and her teeth were white and strong. "She's
been expecting you."

He sat gingerly on a Louis Quinze couch and found that although it was ornate and antique, some upholstered had made it comfortable. He heard a brassy voice in the back of the house and soon Miss Martha strode into the parlor, dressed in khaki pants and shirt. Her head was bound in a colorful kerchief. She had taken gauntlets from her hands, and as she walked she slapped herself on the legs making dust fly.

"Hi, John Sidney. Excuse my appearance. Been riding all over hell and half of Georgia. Della?" Her voice rose stridently. "Bring us a tray of sumpn t' eat. Well ..." she shook his hand with a strong masculine grip. "Glad to see you and I don't beat around the bush. You decided to take me up on my offer?"

"Yes'm."

"Good. Hoped you would. Got to thinking after I blew out of your house the other night. I was a damn fool for acting up like that. Got to thinkin' well ... Hell, maybe people just hadn't appreciated old Hec and my offer to buy his painting might have just string-halted him or sumpin."

"That was it, Miss Martha. Life hasn't been too generous to Uncle Hec, and he didn't recognize your offer for what it was. He thought you were just being kind, and he didn't want that."

"Well, I started out to be kind and found I didn't have to. A welcome surprise, believe me. I never like to find myself in a strain. Now, your money'll be in the bank in the morning. Quit your job yet?"

"Yes ma'am. Yesterday. I registered today."

She swept off her kerchief and he was surprised to see her hair loose. It fell in soft crinkly waves and gave her a softening influence. She was almost lovely in a strong, bold way. "By the way, I didn't hear you drive up."

He smiled. "My feet don't make much noise."

She stared. "You mean to tell me you walked all the way out here from town? And you're wet with sweat. Dammit, why didn't you call me instead of footing it eight miles out here?"

He hesitated for a moment. Why not tell her the truth. He was not ashamed of it. "Miss Martha, maybe you don't realize the full extent of what you're doing for us. It was just something I didn't want to do over the phone. I'd have walked if it'd been twenty miles."

Her eyes softened and grew slightly moist. "You're a good lad, John Sidney. I'm expecting a couple of touchdowns from you Friday night. We've lost three games already, and this Crayville tribe is all ready to lick us again."

He shook his head. "I'm just subbing for Janceys. After all, you can't expect me to step in and dump a regular player out of his job."

She looked at him for a long moment. "You know, I think I'll make you my boy."

John Sidney's face was serious. "That I like."

She looked at him sharply. "You don't remember your mother, son?"

"No Ma'm. Not too well. I was still young when she died."

"Never had a mother. Just a fly by night father and a painting uncle."

"Uncle Hec never thought about it I'm sure, but he's been about the best parent a boy could have. I guess I missed my mother though, without realizing it. I suppose that's why I like girls so … so …" He shrugged. "I like 'em, plenty."

"Did Hec teach you any man-woman ethics?"

"Yes Ma'm. That's one thing he always bore down on. You see he was raised in the South and he got his share of woman respect in his rearing. He's told me times on end that a woman, any woman, should have mans' respect at first meeting. After that it was up to her to deserve it. I've never had the chance or the means to do a lot of dating, but it wasn't because I didn't want to. I've fallen in love a dozen times and all I could do was suffer it out." He considered her silently for a moment. "Now I've really fallen in love. I'm just wondering if I could tell you about it."

"Son, you can tell me anything you want to."

"Yes'm, I think I could, but I'm afraid this will strain your tolerance."

She smiled. "Wrong side of the tracks, hunh? Well, I always say it's what the woman is, rather than where she was born. I've seen some wonderful flowers grow in swampy places."

"This is worse than that. She's part Negro."

"Oh ... dear me," she breathed, but her face didn't register horror or particular surprise.

Della came in with a tray of heavy meat sandwiches and tall frosty tumblers of iced tea. Miss Martha served him bountifully and made small talk until he was eating, then she was silent for a while. Finally she said, "John Sidney, purely because it's the way you affect me, I'm going to reserve any opinion on this love affair until I have a right to utter one. Right now I know nothing but what you've told me, which isn't much. On the surface I'd say you've run head on into a pretty impossible situation, but I never say anything is impossible. Impossibilities usually balk stupid people, but to smart ones, they're just a challenge. Would I know the girl by any chance?"

He shrugged. "I couldn't say. You probably know her foster mother. Everyone does. They call her Mamma Dell. Her last name is Smith."

Miss Martha grunted explosively. "Hell, who don't know Mamma Dell? She slapped life into me right back there in my bedroom. I know Carla and she's a fine woman, a really fine woman. Educated, poised, straight worward, honest, and just between the two of us, about the finest lookin' piece of flesh as you'll find in a days ridin'."

"I got a similar impression," said John Sidney carefully, hoping his face didn't heat up too much, "what little of her I've seen."

"Strictly high caliber," continued Miss Martha, then she sighed, "Yes son, it's gonna be rough, but one thing I can tell you right now, count on me for anything the old woman can do."

John Sidney stopped chewing. He was suffocating, his chest ached and in spite of a valiant effort, a hot rush of tears stung his eyes and started trickling down his cheeks.

"Here." She handed him a paper tissue. "Wipe your eyes and don't be ashamed. Not before me at any rate. Every chance I get, I'm going to make you do that. Good for you. Cleans you out ... like a good dose of salts. I bet you've been a lifetime choking back things like that, that wanted out."

He sighed shudderingly. "Yes'm. I guess I have." He shook his head. "I've seen you twice. Already you've gotten me right down to the quick. Everything happens fast is seems like ... to me anyhow."

She got up and hugged his head. "You're not walking back to town. I'll take you in the Jeep. Lester took the car in this afternoon to have it tuned and the plugs changed. It'll be in town over night. Be nice seein' old Hector ... have to let him know I ain't holdin' a grudge."

By Friday morning Judson Markey could speak in a guarded fashion. "I want out of here," were his first words to Dr. Forrest.

The portly old doctor grinned and thumbed his thick grey moustache. "Sure ... don't they all. I got an interest in this clinic, and we got to keep you here a while to help pay the overhead."

"Do I got to pay it all alone?"

"You talk too much. How do you feel?"

"In the pink. Throat still sore some."

"That's normal. Don't strain your voice. Take it easy for a week, then back to the salt mines for you. Really want to leave?"

"I sure do. These white walls give me the willies."

"Can't have that. Shall I call the missus?"

"No. Call Whitley."

"Why him?"

"He doesn't talk as much as Esther."

Dr. Forrest laughed and picked up the chart from the foot of his bed, glanced over it and wrote a brief sentence at the bottom of the form. "Jud, I wonder if you know how lucky you were?"

"I got a fair head of sense."

Dr. Forrest nodded and replaced the chart. "You were lucky twice. That woman ... they tell me she screamed like a calliope. That brought young Grahame at a dead run ... he couldn't have been over a hundred yards away. If it had been anyone I can possible think of besides an M. D. or Grahame, you'd be as dead as a salted sprat." The doctor shook his head. "I'll have to talk to that boy. Imagine him slitting you open with a pocket knife at exactly the right spot, and inserting a piece of cane for you to breathe through. You ought to play the horses. You couldn't lose."

"Who," Judson wanted to know, "was the woman?"

"Girl name of Carla Smith. School teacher. I know her through her mother who's probably the best midwife in the country. She's even showed me a thing or two. The girl's colored, but I don't guess you'd rair up on your white supremacy right at this moment."

Markey uttered an ugly word. "Right about now, I wouldn't care if she was a one-eyed nightmare. I'm too thankful to her for being alive. Think it over some day Doc, the only people who can appreciate life are those who have shaved it as close as I did.

I think about two minutes more and not even Grahame could have saved me."

"On the contrary," said Dr. Forrest thoughtfully. "The way that boy seems to think, my guess would be that if you hadn't breathed when he inserted that reed, he'd have rolled you over and pumped you with artificial respiration."

Whitley, as predicted talked sparingly, but Esther and Patti had no intention of letting him alone. Patti had innumerable questions to ask and Esther had but one. It was one that could be stretched.

"What was that Negro woman doing at your camp?"

"I've told you some three or four times. She ran out of gas. She came over to borrow some."

"I'll bet that was a pretty sight, her sitting in the back seat, holding your head."

"At that moment I was a little too grateful to her to wonder how it looked. I don't give a tinkers goddamn how it looked, and I've heard all I want to about it."

"I dare say she could have gotten the gas … and anything else she wanted."

"Yes, she could. She still can." He got up. "I'm going to my room, and I don't want to be disturbed."

"Nobody seems to give a damn about me," said Hodge sitting uncomfortably on the sofa, his head immobilized and held still by a leather collar.

"That's a move you started," said Judson evenly. "You don't care much for yourself, so why should anyone else. It was your idea."

"*Judson*," said Esther in a horrified voice.

"I could be wrong on one point. Maybe it wasn't Hodge that started it. Maybe it was you." He made his exit according to plan and left her gasping.

Friday night saw the stands at the school football field filled to the limit, and several hundred spectators stood about unable to find sitting room.

Miss Martha Wyntringham sat in her usual place, wrapped against the chill in a warm blanket, talking animatedly to O'Boyle's wife and two daughters.

Taretown blundered through the first two quarters, giving their supporters little to cheer about, the green quarterback fumbling twice and overshooting on his passes. Worse than that the left halfback allowed a receiver to get behind him and Crayville's only pass went for a touchdown. The extra point attempt was good.

At half time O'Boyle called Janncys and John Sidney aside. "I'm not complaining Jan," he told the boy, "but you just haven't settled in that position yet."

Janncys, a tow headed youth, rather slim and light groaned. "Coach, I just don't have it tonight."

"Yes, I know that. I'm not blaming you. We want that game, and we want it bad. I'm going to play Grahame here in the second half. I just wanted to tell you, and I don't want any ill feelings over it. He's just come with us and you've given us the best you have. I don't want you to feel left out or anything. I'll probably play you back at right half some of the time."

Janncys grinned and slapped John Sidney on the shoulder. "Shucks, Coach, I know I can't swing it like the new recruit. You can't make me sore."

"That's my boy," said O'Boyle. "Grahame, think you can carry the load the second half?"

"Yes sir. I'll do my best."

"That ought to be nearly good enough," he said drily. "Now there's just one thing. As you probably noticed I don't call plays from the bench unless you ask for one. If you get in a tight and

want some advice, face the bench and adjust your headgear. I'll run a guard in with a play for you."

"I find that unusual," commented John Sidney.

"Yeah, I know. I'm peculiar that way. I think it's still the players' game. I ain't above eatin' you out if you boo-boo but it's still your game to play the best you know how."

"Just one thing Coach, I'm not up on all the plays. I'll have to call the ones I am up on."

"That'll be all right. Our line's better than theirs. Go on out there and use your head. That's what I want to see, another thing. I know how you can run. Don't put the load on your backs, use 'em, but use yourself. Wear that option out. That always keeps 'em guessing."

John Sidney used his head and Taretown won by a touchdown.

The men were excited, the crowd was wild, and John Sidney was annoyed. He knew he had played well, but it was something he had gone in there to do, and he didn't enjoy being pounced upon and made over as though he had produced a minor miracle. He ducked into the crowd, and without taking off his uniform, grabbed his clothes and fled.

CHAPTER NINE

He didn't go straight home. He paused in the little growth of woods that bordered the ravine and sat down. His nerves were jumping and he needed time to recover. He had left his helmet in his locker, but otherwise he was dressed out. He allowed himself to calm down by fiddling with the laces of his shoes, taking them off and stripping the tape from his ankles. He slipped his other shoes on without socks and thought the game over from beginning to end, remembering the things he had done wrong, the pass that had turned out lucky for him, but it was bad defense work. After some thirty minutes, he got up and grimaced. He was sore and fatigue was creeping up on him.

Delani raced to meet him as he walked into the back yard and they met in the blade of light the open kitchen door made in the yard. Neither of them were aware that they were being watched.

She caught him by the arms. "I saw … I saw … Oh, you were so wonderful."

John Sidney blushed to the roots of his hair. He didn't care for such open eyed admiration, but decided that from Delani it was all right.

"I was lucky," he mumbled. "How did you see it?"

"I was up on that big oak tree just back of the playing field. Rose and I watched. I just couldn't keep still. I almost fell from the tree."

He sighed and tried to ward off the choky feeling he always got when she was close to him. Her face was animated, her big eyes sparkling and her lips were damp and cream smooth. As the impulse had taken her over at their first meeting, it inundated him this time, and it seemed that he swam into contact with her lips and for a fleeting moment, his head roared out of control and his heart hammered painfully against his ribs.

"*God*," he breatherd, when he could breathe. "This thing it too big for me." He stopped, appalled at what he thought was an exceedingly vacuous remark. She didn't feel that way about it and again tears sprang into her eyes. She clutched him spasmodically and rested her head on his chest.

"It's big," she said in a choked voice. "Big … so big. Maybe it'll take both of us to handle it."

"Will you help?"

"All my life." Her heart stood revealed in her eyes. "*All my life*." A sob shook her and she did a peculiar thing. She caught him about the waist, lifted her lips to his, and when they touched her body went as boneless as a snake and seemed to pour itself into every line of his. Her loins were hot against him, sending a fearful spray of response through him. Then with a strangled sob, she turned and raced into the darkness.

Miss Martha who with Hector had been a breathless witness to the tableau leaped to her feet. "Dammit, come on and get out of here," she whispered stridently, "you old nosy rip." She tugged him into the living room, but John Sidney had seen them through the doorway.

He felt as though he'd never made it up the steps, so shattered by the storm of emotion that had smitten him. He went into the kitchen and dropped his football shoes on the floor. He sat down just as Miss Martha and Uncle Hec came back into the kitchen.

"You," she accused, "look like hell."

He grinned weakly. "I feel sort of shook up ... and don't tell me you didn't see it. I saw you running."

She came to him and hugged his head affectionately. "I couldn't help seeing, son, but I'm your mom and all I can say is that I was also shook up. Right on down to my box ankles."

John Sidney was tired, he was nervous from the tension of the game and sorely shaken by the touch of Delani, her kisses and that fleeting contact with the wonder of her body.

Miss Martha touched him in a very tender spot and with a small sound in his throat, he hugged her around the waist and hid the scalding rush of tears in the front of her coat. She understood and increased the gentle pressure on his head.

Uncle Hec turned around and went back to the living room. He undraped the painting and stared at it, but he didn't see it.

John Sidney relaxed and Miss Martha said, "Now run take your bath and come back so I can tell you what a marvelous game you played tonight."

He stood up and took a stuttering breath. "That was her, Miss Martha."

"Yes ... I assumed as much. I don't think I ever saw a child as lovely as she. I know exactly how you feel. You said she was colored?"

"Yes'm."

"Then she managed to distill the very best of the two races into one person. That's for sure."

He turned to hide a fresh burst of tears and went into the bathroom where he proceeded to take a long hot relaxing bath, and he emerged feeling much better.

Miss Martha was talking to Uncle Hec. "Hector, I sigh for my lost youth. That was the tenderest sight I ever witnessed, those two terribly young things with their life ahead of them and every step studded with bumps and pitfalls. They took a little trip to Heaven tonight, and Hell is yet to come."

"Does it have to come?" he asked puffing thoughtfully on a thick black briar.

"No. I suppose it doesn't *have* to come. Maybe it'll miss them, but why should it?"

She shrugged ponderously. "I think most things come to all people at one time or another. After all, a situation is the product of circumstance. It doesn't think or plan. It's people who cause grief."

"I never said it wasn't," she snapped sharply. "They're people, aren't they?"

"They are people, but I must qualify the remark. They have all the parts one visualizes when referring to people. They, I apologize for being trite, are different in a totally different definition of the word. I suppose," he added with a wry smile, "I sound no different from any father trying to tell about his boy."

Miss Martha laughed. "You should hope everything you do is as easily forgiven. I, too, have that sneakin' feeling that this boy of ours ain't no run of the mill product. That girl ain't either." She frowned, "I got to get behind this and find out who she is. I've heard this and that about her, but I never paid it much mind. I'll have to see Mamma Dell. She's the only one who really knows."

John Sidney came back in, his hair slicked down, in fresh brown slacks and a tan sport shirt. "Hi," he said brightly, while Miss Martha searched his voice and face for effort. She found none. Bouncy youth, she thought.

Miss Martha said, "Well, you and Mike O'Boyle crossed me up and you didn't make a touchdown every time you touched the ball. Instead you handed it off most of the time or passed it. Trouble is, you did it in a way that prevents me from criticizing you. I don't like that. I love to criticize."

John Sidney grinned. "You can criticize the blocks I missed and that pass I let slip through my hands."

"Yes and look what you did with that. Damn if I'll ever know how you got off the ground in time to catch it in the air. Anyhow, I was well pleased with you. Your money's in the bank and all you have to do is go down there and sign the card so they'll know your signature ... and get yourself a checkbook ... How're you fixed for clothes?"

"He can cover his nakedness," said Uncle Hec, "but barely. His suit is too small. He hasn't worn it in a year. It was too small when he stopped wearing it."

Miss Martha put a hand over John Sidney's. "Son, go down to Fleets tomorrow and get yourself some clothes, shoes, shirts ... everything you need. If you're going to pass as my relative, then you got to live the part."

His smile very nearly trembled. "Thanks," he said huskily. "I guess I'd better go to bed. I'm bushed."

He left, and Uncle Hec brandished a gin bottle. "Join me?"

"I'll precede you," she barked, and taking the bottle, downed a stiff dollop.

Uncle Hec watched her and in his breast was reborn a tiny coal of warmth that had guttered out long ago. That there was enough coal left to rekindle into a flame, he did not believe.

Patti Markey had watched the game, the last half, that is, with bated breath. John Sidney Grahame grew in stature from a mere man who'd given her father a hand in need, to a veritable god.

The next day she was so full of his sensational play that Hodge had growled with disgust and left her presence. Judson half heard her, a habit he was cultivating as a bulwark against the women in his house, but enough of it struck through to make him realize that it was the lad who had given him such sorely needed help that she was talking about.

"Invite him to dinner," he had said, half jokingly. "I've a few words to say to him myself."

It was no joke to Patti, and after being assured by her mother that the board would be full and festive, she appropriated the second family car and drove at an illegal rate of speed to John Sidney's house, after asking and getting directions from a grocery store where they bought food.

He met but didn't particularly care for Mrs. Markey. He considered her vapid and shallow. He met Hodge and his previous contact with him had already developed dislike, intense dislike.

"They tell me you're the big hero," said Hodge, with a thinly veiled sneer.

"I did all right," said John Sidney, his eyes steady on the other's.

"Lucky for you I was out of the line up, with this neck."

"I understand you were in the line-up last year when they played Crayville."

Hodge turned bright red. He didn't like to be reminded that last year they had lost twenty-six to eighteen, three of his passes having been intercepted and run back for touchdowns.

Patti saved Hodge further embarrassment by coming back into the room. "Dad says would you come to his room. He's not feeling in the pink."

John Sidney went into the handsome room, with its masculine furniture, heavy and comfortable.

"Ah … my valued young friend. Come in. I'm Judson Markey, as if you didn't know."

"Nice to meet you, sir," said John Sidney taking the proffered hand, "under happier circumstances."

"Beat it, Patti," said Judson. "You wouldn't be interested in this."

She pouted and flounced out, twisting her hips in a manner that made John Sidney's blood race a little faster.

Judson looked at the departing figure of his daughter and sighed. "Some likely lad will take care of that twist, or I miss my bet." He smiled wrily. "Sounds like hell for a father to say that, doesn't it?"

"I think you took her twist for an unspoken invitation," said John Sidney.

"What would you take it for?"

John Sidney smiled. "If I agreed with you, I wouldn't be likely to say so, would I?"

"No. I guess you wouldn't. Son, I asked you in here because I had an idea this might embarrass you. I'll make it as brief as possible. You handed me my life back, and for what it's worth, Judson Markey is a friend of yours. Now I've said it and that's the end of it. I've asked around and I understand that you and your uncle are not in the best financial position, what with you going to school and him ..." He paused.

"And him not working," finished John Sidney.

"Yes. Well, that's not my business and I'm sure he has his reasons. What I wanted to say is that anytime you're pressed or even before that, I'm ready, willing and able to give you a hand just as far as you need it. I don't take you for a fool, so I feel I can make the offer without a lot of qualifications. If I seem overly grateful, it's because I am overly grateful. You have to come as close to the grave as I did to realize in full what I mean."

"Yes sir. As much as I can I think I know what you mean. I was there working on you, watching the light go dim."

"All right. You can go now if you wish. I stay in here as much as I can because those two women of mine wear me out. One moment. Are you acquainted with the colored woman who helped you?"

"Acquainted ... yes. Not well, but acquainted. She lives across the ravine from me."

Judson nodded abstractedly. "She seems sort of dim in my mind right now and yet ..." He hesitated.

John Sidney said, "She's quite a person, you know."

Judson cut him a quick glance. "Yes ... I've had that impression lingering on me ever since ..."He stopped and frowned. "I invited her to eat with me that day." He looked at John Sidney for some sight of disapproval, and saw none. There was another flick of the eyes. "I just wanted you to know."

"I've talked to her, sir. She wanted me to know, too."

"Know what?"

"Why she was there."

"What did she tell you?"

"That her car had run out of gas. She went to your camp to borrow some."

Judson chuckled rustily. "You know ... I'd forgotten why she had come, originally."

"Why do you say, originally?"

The older man turned red. "Damn," he breathed, and looked away.

"Like I told her, you don't owe me any explanation of anything sir. It is none of my business why she was there." John Sidney smiled. "However, both of you, striving to make is seem as nothing, which I had already decided anyway, managed to give the impression that it wasn't as casual a meeting as you both pretend."

Judson went red again. "We talk much but not well ... the girl and me. However, you appear to be rather mature. Actually, I didn't want you to think about it too much, because not for the world would I have it get out that I was entertaining women at my camp. Not for me, mind you. Every day that passes I care less what the public thinks of me. I wonder how in the hell I was *ever* so concerned."

"It's the natural thing that a man with a family wouldn't want scandal attached to his name."

"I suppose so, but my concern was for the girl. She *did* come there for gas ..." Judson shook his head. "It sounds daft when one says it out loud."

"Maybe that's because so many things felt sound silly when spoken. Words have their limitations. Man's inner self probably does too, but its capacity is so much greater than his ability to describe it."

Judson smiled benignly. "You speak as a man of mature years. How do you know?"

"Because it had happened to me."

"You ... I wouldn't have suspected it."

"I'm in love with Carla's sister."

Judson sat bolt upright in bed. "My God ... you too?"

"Yes sir. That's how I know you can feel something that is impossible to describe. I can't tell you what she does to me because I hardly know myself. I do know that it happens when I'm with her and the world seems to fly apart ... me with it."

"Yes, that's the way it was. She touched me, just a friendly handshake. I was lonely and wanted her to eat with me. We shook hands and it was like touching a live wire. I almost came apart too." Judson grinned crookedly. "Looks like we're in the same boat, sort of. Of course, I have a wife. That is she passes as my wife. She's something less then what I'd expect a wife to be. I came to this conclusion about a week ago. I wonder why I'm telling a boy all this. A boy not much, if any, older than my own son, whom I'd tell nothing. I guess circumstances have made us blood brothers. One of these circumstances Patti will not like. She's rather chosen you for herself."

"I'm not cold to her attraction. She's quite a flame."

Judson lifted an eyebrow. "At which you might not refuse to warm your hands."

John Sidney lifted his shoulder. "Either I tell the truth or I shut up. After all, you're her father."

Judson put his hands beneath his head. "All right, John Sidney. Looks like we have no secrets. As a father, I'd want nothing of a tragedy to happen to Patti."

"Nothing will, sir. Not if I know what you mean. Shall I stay away from her?"

"No. I lay down no rules. You sound like you know your way around. I want no scandal, I want no tragedy, hate, bitterness … things like that."

"Hate and bitterness," replied John Sidney presciently, "always seem to come from tragedy or scandal. I can't predict what any single person may do long range … how they may react, how they may think."

"Neither can I," said Judson, peering into the distant nowhere. "Neither can I, John Sidney."

"May I say one other thing, sir?"

"Of course."

"She has a tough philosophy … Carla I mean. We discussed you. She is aware of all the angles where you're concerned. Her philosophy amounts to this. 'Take what you can, in any way you can. If you can't have all, take a part … any part, and be glad of it. If you can't join it, beat it.' That's it with my own slant from what she told me."

Judson felt a suffocating feeling in his chest and he stroked his throat. "My throat hurts," he said in a soft peculiar voice. "Get out of here and let me think."

After dinner, without asking permission of anyone, Patti suggested a ride. After a bare second's hesitation John Sidney accepted. The fact that Delani had kissed him, impulsively the first time they had met didn't seem to impress as much as the fact that Patti slid over and snuggled close to him before they were even out of town. He could feel the ecstatic warmth of her left breast as it pressed into his upper arm and tingled from the touch.

Patti was now a changed person. In some ways she seemed childish, when she spoke in a conspiratorial hush, and in other ways projected the thesis that this was an entirely clandestine thing, promising all sorts of delectable variations before the date was over.

"Let's ride up to Dad's camp," she said with a giggle. I want to see what's so great about it. He can't wait to get back to it."

John Sidney agreed, but did not remark on several things he could think of that made the camp attractive to Judson.

"Do you like to smooch, John Sidney?" she asked with a whispery laugh.

"Um … well …"

"I mean *really* smooch. Not any of your childish pecking stuff. I mean throw a real job."

John Sidney allowed a delightful anticipatory chill race over him for a moment in perfect freedom. "A real job …" He thought for a moment. "And how far does this *real* job go?"

The question surprised a quick burst of quizzical mirth from her. "Oh … I don't know. How far is far?"

"If you're an experienced smoocher, you must have run into some situations where a halt was called for."

"Halt … what halt?"

"Oh, then you do know how far far is."

She sobered a little and shook her head. "No … I really don't know."

"Then I think the place for you is home right about now."

"Oh don't *you* turn out to be a square," she flared hotly.

John Sidney was momentarily halted. Either this girl had taken him out with rather mature intent, or she was so far out of her depth that she didn't know what she was sounding like.

"A square" he replied, "is a honest figure with four right angles. Compared to a circle which can be stretched and mashed into a variety of shapes and never crack a boundary. I don't care what you call me and that term square is a part of the language of wet-eared adolescents who amuse each other with such cuteness, indicating about two years from the doll-baby stage.

"You talk like a combination school teacher and preacher," she sneered. "I bet for all your mature ways, I could show you a thing or two."

"I doubt it" he said softly. "An approach to maturity in association, an approach to the edge of the cliff where smooching had been taken care of and the next thing, the only thing left you"d scream and cry and run home to Mamma."

"You couldn't make *me* cry uncle" she flared. "I know your type. You're all mouth and nothing else. Stop the car ... I dare you."

He stopped the car and she fell into his arms and drew his face close to hers. "Please let's don't fight, John Sidney."

He smiled. "Is this fighting?" He said his mouth into hers, twisted it expertly and forced her lips wide. His right hand stroked gently the fine lines of her back and across the delectable swell of her hip, then back to her face where he gently eased her hair from her ear and temple, then stroked the back of her neck where he urged her closer still.

Her jaws slackened appreciably and availed him of the honeyed cavern of her mouth, the hesitant activity of her tongue. His own tasted the tender under surfaces of her lips and wrung a deep fundamental groan from her.

Then without warning, she went to pieces. She tore her mouth from his and buried her face in the cloth of his coat and wept with a harsh released bitterness that he couldn't understand, but later thought maybe he did. He expected such a kiss to shock her, but he had no way of knowing, although later he guessed, that he must have typified the man in her dreams, dreams she had nurtured for a long time, then to have them explode into being was a little more than her youth could stand.

She sat up and shook her head, then held her face with her hands for a moment. "All right, so you're right. I couldn't take it." She sobbed jerkily. "Well, doesn't that make you all happy and victorious and superior and a complete stinker?"

"No."

"Why?"

"Because I *knew*. You didn't. You just thought you knew. Most things come up that way. I've been wrong. Most young people are a lot of the time. They need teaching. You were wrong. I taught you. Now you know. If you learned a lesson you're ahead of the game. If you didn't, then you're in sad shape. Some people can be taught, some can't. It's up to you."

She held her hands to her face for a moment and sobbed. "What makes me so mad I could bite and scream is that I cried ... I'm still crying and I don't know why."

"Shall I tell you?"

"Oh ... do" she said sarcastically.

"You're wrong, Patti. You put your fifty yard dash emotions to the job of running a mile. They pooped on you. It happens all the time."

"All right, Socrates. I guess you want to take me home now."

"Not unless you want to go home. If you do, I'll take you."

She crumpled against him for a moment, holding his arm hard. "John Sidney ... please don't take me home now. Maybe

I'm not as bad as I've shown up to be … I mean … maybe I won't crumple up again."

"To the camp?

"To the camp." She crept into the circle of an offered arm and clung to him tightly all the way.

They pulled up in front of the camp and he stopped the car. She shivered a little and held to him.

"Let's don't get out, just yet" she said in a small voice.

He nodded and twisted in the seat and bent his head until his lips were inches from hers. She made a throaty little sound and offered him her mouth. John Sidney was not, in his own opinion, an expert kisser, but he was expert at following the dictates of his urges, and he left her weak and huddled against him. His own blood coursed through his veins in a roaring cataract.

"I didn't … come apart that time" she said finally.

"You did fine. I was the one who came apart that time."

She gave an ecstatic little cry and offered him her mouth again. Her breasts were restless electrodes, burning his chest and the action of his hands stroking the exciting symmetry of her back made her body writhe and seek to find a counterpart with which to mingle. She didn't cry when he released her this time, but she held him close and strove mightily to regain her breath and balance. He caught her to him and kissed the line of her throat, the shell-pink lobes of her ears, then downward until he reached the exciting foothills of her proud breasts. She screamed softly and clutched him with dispairing strength.

He raised his aim and found her lips again and this time it was a ravenous attack, a feeding of one upon another. His left hand dropped lower, found the alabastine surface of a thigh and she went wild.

Her body bowed itself into a fabulous sickle as the torment-ing hand rose higher and sensation screamed through her nerves like a forest fire. Finally his hand stopped. She held him with all her might for a few seconds, then collapsed and wept with tired quietness. He held her until her weeping subsided. Her hand crept downward, found his and held it close.

She tilted her face until it was close to his. "Please tell me what to do."

"You ought to go home, Patti."

She shivered and pressed his hand closer. "No ... I don't want to go home." In the starlight her bared thigh was a shimmering shaft of the purest marble.

"All right" he whispered. "You tell me what you want me to do."

Her clutch was spasmodic. "I think you know. Let's go into the cabin."

CHAPTER TEN

"It's your first sufferin', chile," said Mamma Dell kindly as she patted Delani's glistening hair. The girl sat at her feet, resting her head against Mamma Dell's knee. "It's your first, but not your last so you can just bunch up your muscle and bear it. It ain't never as bad as it feels, first off. You'll feel like you was about to die a thousand times, but you'll live out the time what the Master put you here to live."

Delani sighed lugubriously. "But it makes me sick. I shouldn't want him that way. I shouldn't want anything the way I want him. It's just something bigger than me. I can't seem to do anything about it."

"Young love don't make for doin' much" Mamma Dell reminded her. "Mostly it's sufferin'."

Delani turned and looked into the old woman's seamed face. "It'll happen Mamma Dell, I know it will. I won't be able to help it, and he won't either."

"What'll happen?" asked Mamma Dell, a chill around her heart because she knew well.

Delani's eyes didn't waver a fraction. "When he touches me I go all watery inside and deep inside me I want him so that I ache, like a toothache." She placed her hand with out shame. "I want him here."

Mamma Dell nodded slowly. "I know that. I know it because in my day I was a pretty high stepper myself. I know you can't help it and honey, Mamma Dell can't tell you what to do. That's sumpn between you and yourself, and him. you're some older'n I was my first time."

"Is it wrong Mamma Dell?"

Mamma Dell contrived to sigh and chuckle at the same time. "So they say, honey. So they say."

"What do you say?"

Mamma Dell thought that over for a long time before she answered. "It's a prickly question to talk about. Take me, I was smart. Didn't anything ever happen to me that I didn't want to happen. I never was no loose woman to go to the bushes with anything that came along. I was *some* choosy. Most gals gonna sport around some when they're young, but just remember this. A man don't want no tramp for a wife. If he do then he ain't worth no woman marry'n, cause he ain't got no pride. Them's the sort of men what'll rustle up trade for their own wives. They ain't got no more principle than a boar coon."

She took out a thin cherott and lit it. "The Master give you what you got. How you use it is sumpn you got to decide for yourself."

"But I do want you to understand the difference. I'm no loose woman. I love one man. He loves me. He wants me. I want him. I don't want anyone else!

" 'Course you ain't no loose woman" snapped Mamma Dell crossly. "You ain't got the first notion what a loose woman's like.'" Tears came into the old woman's eyes. "Lord have mercy on us, chile. This is one time when Mamma Dell ain't got no orders. Must seem strange … me not havin' no orders, no rules. This here is the wrong place for sumpn like this to happen. There is two jillion stumbles and twice that many falls comin' for you. Ever' one of 'em will hurt like a wasp sting. You say he's startin' school?"

"Yes'm."

"Then ever' white gal in school gonna be after him. I know. He's too good lookin', he's quiet and he minds him owns business. Some of them flibberty gibbety gals ain't gonna like that part of 'im, but they'll learn. You got competition."

Delani grinned. "You make me feel better. I don't care about competition. It doesn't bother me at all. I couldn't be wrong, Mamma Dell. He wants me just as bad as I want him."

Mamma Dell looked into the far distance. They were in love. Love wouldn't wait. "Wanta do sumpn for me, Delani?"

"Yes'm."

"Tell the boy to come see your old mammy. I think I oughta talk to him."

"Yes'm I'll tell him."

Whitely had visited and because Judson was overpowered by a burning desire to talk. Whitley now knew all. He grinned and said, "Well … unbrace yourself. What'd you expect me to do? Bite you?"

Judson relaxed sweating. "No … I know you're a dyed in the wool southerner, and I didn't know just how you'd take it."

"Don't let these dyed in the wool southerners fool you, Jud. Somewhere in the dim past some plantation owner fed to teeth with his pale complaining New England wife who couldn't unbend if her life depended on it, went out and saw a gleam in some dark skinned nymph's eyes and followed it. He found the new bed a sight of improvement over the one he left. Result? A pure Negro is next to impossible to find. Don't ask me how we reconcile the apparent paradox. I'm not prepared to answer that. We won't sit in the same bus seat with one, but then that is another matter entirely."

"You're being faintly heretical" said Judson, with a grin.

"Yes, I know. Heresy often creeps into cases like this. One of these days if I get drunk enough I might tell you of my own peculations across the line."

"You, too?"

"Me, too. I won't say how it racked me up when at last, seeing that there was nothing in it for her but clandestine love, never position or respect or future, she wisely married. I won't say what happened afterward, time and time again with others. In fact, I don't think I'll say anything at all."

"Bully for you, you close mouthed cuss.

Esther burst into the room the instant Whitley left. "I *wish* you'd look at *this*."

He looked. What he saw were a pair of very expensive panties trimmed in very expensive lace. They seemed somewhat the worse for wear, "Well?"

"She *did* it."

"Who ... did what?"

"Patti. These she wore with that ... that ... Grahame *creature* last night. *I knew* something was the matter with her. She's so dreamy eyed and so stunned she can't *talk*. She doesn't even *listen* when I talk."

"That last is a pure defense mechanism born of habit."

"I don't care for your sarcasm."

"Then leave me be. I'm tired."

"*You* mean to lay there when your daughter has been out giving herself to that ... *nobody*?"

"So she's my daughter now. Look Esther, you were young once. I can almost remember it."

"She *did* it" she shrilled. "I *know* she did. I just *know* it."

"There's one thing certain" he snapped, losing his temper, "she exercised greater taste than Hodge has in his amours. Apparently she didn't force Grahame or harm him physically. I find it odd that you take up for Hodge and bend logic until it is unrecognizable to make him look good and the first suspicion you have that touches Patti, you blow up and accuse her of all sorts of things. That, to me, passes belief."

"Oh … you're *impossible* … *totally* impossible."

"What I said stands. Why the hurrah about Patti and the opposite attitude when Hodge gets in trouble with the police?"

"You wouldn't know how a parent feels about their children. Not you!"

"In that, you're probably right. I've never been a father except technically. I don't feel that I have children. I feel that they're strangers living in my house, coming to me for money with meal-time regularity. You opposed every move I ever made toward discipline, always quoting some slimy ass who puts himself up as an expert on child psychology. Well, they're *your* product. It's your bed. You made it, so you go lie in it. And don't come to me about it."

"You mean you're *not* going to talk to that Grahame *thing* about her?"

"No. I admire that Grahame thing a great deal, too much to badger him about something that was probably not his fault. It just happens that this Grahame *thing* you mention, single hand-edly, saved my life. That, I know has never impressed you worth two cents. It impressed me. I value my life."

"You *would*," she cut at him.

"Yes. I'm peculiar that way … not being a cat. Now if you don't mind get the hell out and leave me alone. I'm tired and my throat hurts."

Esther flounced out in a mercurial rage and Judson, his breast a battleground for a host of emotions managed a dry chuckle.

John Sidney, though wise beyond his years had much to learn of women. He had not known that one of the most adhe-sive conditions known to man develops when he has loved a woman well. Patti became his shadow. When there were football trips, she was there. She dogged his footsteps at noon recess. She never missed a football practice and always had the offering of dinner, a ride in her car or anything that could entice him into her company. Her body she gave with a passion that was almost frightening and her appetite was enormous.

Mike O'Boyle, not having been born yesterday, began to frown when he saw them together. He knew what too much love could do to a man's stamina, by making him lose sleep, if nothing else.

One day after practice, the coach, who was now aware that the only thing between Taretown High and a lousy season was one John Sidney Grahame, took him aside for a fatherly talk. "Look kid, I may be jumpin' the gun. I know I'm sticking my nose into your private affairs, but I just would like to say a word of warning."

"Yes, sir."

O'Boyle was uneasy under the steady eyes of the boy. "Now don't get me wrong. I don't say that there's anything between you and the Markey girl. Maybe there ain't a thing but this I know. I've been watching and if there's nothing between you, then it's your doing. She'd let you have it in a minute. That's between you and her. My point is, too much of that sort of thing can ruin your game. I had to play her brother, Hodge, because of pressure and the fact that he is a good ball handler, but I've seen him go on the field lap-legged. He wasn't worth a tupenny damn. I don't want to see that happen to you."

John Sidney nodded. "I know what you mean. How does a man get rid of a girl like her? She's in my hair."

"You should have got rid of her that first night, son. If you ever throw a good lay, then they're always hanging around for an encore. It never fails. Sure, they get in your hair, but don't ask me how to get her out. There ain't no formula that I know about. If you're leery about telling her off, then duck her."

John Sidney was inclined to agree, but he hardly knew how to tackle the job. He enjoyed her company and their lovemaking was a strong magnet. It would take some will power to send her away, and if he did, how did he know he wouldn't want to go back? That, manifestly, would not be fair.

CHAPTER ELEVEN

M iss Martha came to dinner. Uncle Hec had quite outdone himself and had a chicken pie in the oven that was giving out a heavenly smell.

"And I brought some sparkling burgundy" said Miss Martha, unwrapping a large bottle of rich red wine with a wired cork.

"That'll make this pie the noble dish it was intended to be" said Uncle Hec, looking through the glass of the oven. "Ten more minutes."

Miss Martha tilted the gin bottle and took a hefty swig, wiping her mouth with the back of her hand "Hec, what's with John Sidney and this Markey chirp?"

Uncle Hec frowned. "If I had the right, or could think of something, I'd talk to him about her. He, I'm afraid, practically lives in her underwear. I don't think it would amount to much, but you know a woman who has been wonderfully and poetically loved."

"Yes. They stay around under foot, hoping to get trodden again. I just hope he doesn't get her in trouble, because that would mean trouble all around. Markey'd come blasting around insisting that he make an honest woman out of her and the fat would be in the fire but good."

Uncle Hec shrugged. "He has been well and thoroughly instructed from that angle. I'm sure he has sense enough to mind what he's about. You weren't thinking solely of him and the Markey girl, were you?"

"No. Actually I was thinking of the dear child across the ravine. I've put it off as long as I can. I've got to see Mamma Dell."

"Then you don't think he's taken a tumble for Patti Markey?"

"No. I don't know Judson but I know his wife, and she's an outsized shot of morphine in skirts. She's a crashing, witless bore. She chaps my ass four ways from Sunday. I've gotten an earful about that boy of his, and none of it's good. I guess he"ll think twice before attacking anyone else. That business intrigues me no end. I'd love to know the Samaritan who jerked that knot in his neck." She took another swig of gin. "I'm depending on John Sidney's good sense and good taste. I can't see him falling for Patti. I wonder what Delani thinks about it? She's bound to know."

He nodded. "She came over the other evening. He was gone, naturally. She talked for a while, then left. She didn't ask about him. Didn't mention his name. I could feel it though. She either knows or will know."

"Yes, and she's not likely to care for the situation too much, especially when she's not in much of a position to say anything about it." She sighed. "You know, I'm actually enjoying feeling concerned over that boy. The rascal has crept under my hide like a chigger. You know Hec, woman was placed on earth to breed and reproduce. It's a hell of a wallop to find out you're sterile as a spayed possum. It'll magnify every neurosis and tic you ever had or heard of. Emotional starvation is almost as bad as the lack of food." Her eyes grew tender. "No, I've got me a boy and dammit, I'm as tickled as a preacher with a tray full of money."

Uncle Hec laughed. "I had some mixed opinions of you once, Martha … excuse me if I seem familiar, but I am older than you, you know. Now, however, I see a truly fine woman, a lonely woman who likes people of her own choice. And if I may be bold again, a surpassingly beautiful woman."

"Oh, go to hell" she said, turning pink. "I'm as big as the side of a gin house and I'm noisy. I never learned to act like a lady."

"You didn't have to" he said softly. "You were born one."

"Oh Hec, shut up. You'll have me giggling like a school girl before you know it. Now about that painting. Still feel I'm just trying to throw away good money?"

"Not any more. I'm sorry the way we acted that night. I guess we were overwhelmed. You can be pretty overwhelming, you know."

"What would be a good price?"

"Martha, please believe me, I can't sell you that picture."

"Indeed, and why not?"

"Because you've been too fine to us, both of us. I'd feel like a sheep killing dog if I took money from you for a daub that's nothing but a sheet of canvas with oils spilled on it, of questionable value."

She eyed him with such intensity that he felt slightly seared. "That's right. Canvas, oils and Hector Grahame. What's any painting, you dimwitted ass, but paint, canvas and the artist? On that painting is you. Every interpretation of every blade of grass, every bird, every tree is you. That lovely woman is the way you see women. That's the way a beautiful woman should look to you. That's the way it is. It is as much a portrait of you as it is the woman, the birds and the trees."

Uncle Hec examined the pie to hide the dampness about his lids. "You can have it, Martha, but please don't try to pay me for it. I only wish I had something that really deserved you. I don't. The canvas is just a gesture."

"What else could you give me" she snorted heatedly. "Money? Hell, I got enough of that to burn this house down. Nothing anyone gives me amounts to a damn except the spirit of giving. I'll accept the picture but I don't agree that it's the only thing you have to give.

"What else?"

"I leave that to your vaunted imagination" she said abruptly, and tilted the gin bottle again.

John Sidney came in then and Uncle Hec took the pie from the oven. It was crispy brown and smelled delicious.

They ate and Uncle Hec popped the cork from the bottle of wine and poured three glasses. He passed them around and said, "To us, the future and to the handsomest woman in Burl County."

John Sidney grinned and lifted his glass. "I double that."

They drank and Miss Martha covered her confusion noisily. "That's all for you, young man" she brayed. "You're in training and don't you forget it, if you haven't already. What's with this Patti critter?"

"She hangs around" said John Sidney, somewhat embarrassed.

"So she does, and while she's hanging around, what happens to Delani?"

He put down his glass and stared at her. "I never even think of them in the same ..." He shook his head. "There's no competition between them. Funny, until you brought it up, I'd never even thought of them together."

"Then you'd better think of them together. You're a nitwit if you think Delani doesn't know."

"Gosh, I hadn't thought of that. I haven't seen Delani lately either."

"Now" warned Miss Martha, "before you start pricking yourself with the icepick, I'd better tell you something. Man being male and subject to all sorts of glandular disturbances often forgets one girl momentarily while listening to the pipes of pan played by another female, if you'll pardon the clumsy analogy. Patti, the wily heifer filled you up with Patti. You being young heeded that which was at hand and it is at hand unless I miss my guess."

John Sidney turned scarlet, and Miss Martha bellowed, with laughter. "See, what did I tell you. Just watch yourself son. It'd be hell to become a father before you got to be a husband."

The thought gave John Sidney a chill making him recall an accident which had caused him concern, but it had turned out safely. Would another, or a third? He felt a momentary panic.

When he finished his dinner he excused himself and went out of the house.

Miss Martha chuckled. "Well, I guess I gave him something to think about. Bet you a dime he'll find Delani. Another dime he'll make up to her this dereliction of loyalty."

Uncle Hec looked at her soberly. "I find it odd that you take this attitude. You must know what an impossible thing any union between them will be. You must see the tragedy ..."

"I see nothing of the sort" she snapped. "I've got a feeling about her that I can't put my finger on. I've *got* to talk to Mamma Dell. Hector, I've seen the girl. I was a lot more skeptical when he told me about her than I am now. I just have never seen anything to equal her. That girl *looms*. She carries a *presence* with her that's like a radium glow. I don't care what you say about her possible ancestry. Anyhow, take Carla for instance, and that maid of mine Della. Ever see two finer specimens in your life? No, you haven't seen Della, which is just as well. She's like me, and doesn't have any morals to speak of. That's why we get along so well. Nope, I fail to find and tragedy ... and I'm sensitive to such things. Another thing Hec, she could *pass* for white anywhere ... and I've got more strategems up my sleeve than a commanding general."

He sighed heavily. "I hope you never need them, but I'm afraid you will."

He found her dressed in faded denims and a blue jacket, seated on the milk can where he had first seen her. A tremendous flood of guilt poured down upon him and he felt unsure, embarrased.

"Hello Delani."

"Hello John Sidney. I haven't seen you lately."

"No." He stopped, he'd only make matters worse trying to explain. "I'm sorry about that."

"Is she nice?"

"Who?"

"Patti Markey."

He flushed and swallowed. Even under pressure he couldn't lie. "Yes, she's nice."

She smiled. "I'm glad you said that. I wouldn't want you to tell me a lie. If she wasn't nice, you wouldn't forget so easily."

"I did not forget you" he said with flat emphasis. "I'm here right now. Doesn't that prove it?"

"I'm sorry. I shouldn't have said that. There's nothing abnormal about you dating a nice girl."

"Thanks. It would be pretty hard to explain. It just sort of happened. I helped her father when he choked on a fishbone and they invited me to dinner. That's how it started."

She stood up. "I have a favor to ask."

"Certainly."

"Mamma Dell would like to talk to you. Will you come see her?"

"Of course." He felt a cold lump in his stomach. What could the old woman want? He had seen her, but had never spoken to her.

He was ushered into her room. "Mamma Dell, this is Mr. Grahame."

She might have been sixty five or ninety. It was hard to tell but she was still hale and healthy, and her clothes as neat as a pin. Her face brightened. "I'm right proud to meet you, son. Have a chair. Delani, bring the rocker."

He sat down gingerly and felt another chill as Delani left the room leaving them alone.

Mamma Dell lit a cherott and sat back. "Son, I hope you won't mind an old dark woman talkin' to you."

"No, Ma'm. I don't mind at all." He felt easier.

"Ever since the other day when I tole Delani I'd like to talk to you I been settin' here wonderin' what I'd say. I know what I want to say, but I ain't the best in world with words. Now I can snatch a baby before a cat can wash his face, but talkin' ain't never been my long suit. 'Course, I guess you know it's about you and Delani."

"Yes Ma'm. Ithought that."

"Well, you're a white boy. She passes for colored. You ever thought about that?"

"Yes'm, I've thought about it."

'And what come outa your thinkin'?"

He thought for a moment,' then lifted frank eyes to hers. "May I call you Mamma Dell?"

" 'Course you can. Ever'body does … white and black. I've near 'bout forgot what my real name is."

"Mamma Dell, I know I'm pretty young to talk like a man but I can only say what I feel. I never felt about anyone else the way I feel about Delani. There isn't even any good way to describe it, but to answer you question, I don't care if she is colored."

"Spoke like a man." She nodded vigorously. "Since you done all that thinkin' you must have thought how such a thing would go here.'"

"Yes, I've thought of that too. What came out of that thinking was that this isn't the only place in the world."

"You'd do that, for her?"

He sighed and dropped his eyes. "There isn't anything I wouldn't do for her. For the last few days I've been going around with another girl." He explained the situation fully then added, "I suppose Delani didn't like it too much."

"No, she wouldn't like it, but a man's a man, and she's got to find that out some day. You didn't do nuthin' against her by goin' with the girl." Mamma Dell tapped a long ash from her cheroot. "Son, Delani talks pretty straight to me. If you two keep on seein' each other and the Master knows I'd never raise my hand to stop it, ever think what could happen, what's just as sure to happen as you two keep seein' each other?"

He turned pink. "I've thought about that."

"You got 'nuff will power to stay on your side of the line?"

He shook his head slowly. "I'm afraid not. I think you'd rather know the truth."

She smiled widely, revealing a mouthful of yellowed but strong teeth, her own. "Son, I like you better by the minnit. Wouldn't a thing but the truth of got by me right now.

"I'm too old and too smart to try to tell children what to do and what not to do. They going to foller their natures and all the talk in the world ain't going to stop 'em. All does, some knows, some don't. Them as knows, they got a chance. Them as don't, ain't got a holler down a well …"

He was silent for a while. "Mamma Dell, I'm glad I talked to you."

"Thank you, son. I only did what I thought right."

"Nothing you told me changed anything. I'm just glad we think alike about it."

"Thirty years ago I'd of told you sumpn very different. I'da told you I'd send for the sherriff you got my girl in trouble. Sendin' for the sheriff don't do anybody any good and it advertises it."

"What is your opinion of me dating other girls"?

"I think it's good. You're young and she's young. You think heavy but you know light. Neither one of you got any notions how you'll, feel a year from now."

"Delani, she's not going to like that."

"See her when you can. You live close. You could see her for a few minutes nearly every day. You both know you can't take her around and she won't 'spect it. Tell her when she asks you. Other'n that, keep your mouth shut. Men break their back when nature says one thing and some other pressure goes against it. Somehow and somewhere along the line nature and morals got their wires crossed. Just remember this son, nature always wins. It might kill you or run you crazy, but it's gonna win every time. Be what you can and don't fret over what you can't be."

He waited for dismissal, wondering if she was through, hoping she wasn't. Her talk had fascinated him, educated him and made him feel freer than he had felt in a long time.

"Well, you run along now and any time you get any vexations bring 'em to Mamma Dell. She done had some, heard of some more and seen 'em all. They ain't never as bad as they look, first glance."

He got up and offered a strong shapely hand She grasped it, her own grip that of a man. "Thanks a million, Mamma Dell."

"Go along with you" she made shooing motions with her hands. "That gal's out there somewhere waitin' for you."

Carla met him first. "Mr. Grahame, could I speak with you for a moment?"

"Of course, and the answer is yes. I've seen him. He's doing fine."

In the mellow light of a low powered bulb he could see the rich stain of blood on her creamy cheek. "That was a low blow" she said with a half laugh. "But that was what I wanted to ask."

"We talked about you."

"You did? What did he say?"

"I'm no good at repeating conversations, but …" He stopped, his face serious. "Carla, he's in love with you. I'm saying this without any certain knowledge. It was just the way he acted, the way he talked. I'd bet on it."

Her hands flew to her face and she pressed her fingers into her eyes. "I think I've been half hoping maybe it'd all be something I imagined. That maybe it'd all die out and nothing would come of it."

"Are you serious?" he asked softly.

She took her hands down, her eyes red and suffering. "No," she said bitterly. "I'm a steam driven liar. Maybe what I mean is … I thought that was probably what would happen, hoping with all my might it wouldn't. Mr. Grahame, what must I do?"

"The first thing I'd do" he said with noticable earnestness, "is consider what the future holds for you if you do get together again. You're intelligent enough to know just what you face, what you stand to get out of it, and what the game will be like. I have a feeling that he'll be yours all right, but you won't be able to own him."

Her eyes flared. "I told you once, I'll take what I can get. Let those who own him take care of that kind of possession." Her nose narrowed and breath whistled into her nostrils. "Am I being smug? Am I being stupid when I feel that whatever is to be mine of him, I feel certain will come to me?"

He shook his head. "I don't think so. I have no proof, only what he said, and the way he said it."

"Then I'll *take* what's mine. The others can have their position, their possession, his name, whatever else they want like that. I, too, will have possession, one peculiar to me my very own. I'd be happier with that than nothing. I will *not* be made unhappy by what I can't have."

He smiled. "In that case I'd run out of gas again."

Her dimples deepened and her face lighted and glowed until he took in a sibilant breath, enthralled by what he saw.

"You know, that's a very good idea."

"It took you a long time" said Delani as she sat waiting for him on the milk can.

"I enjoyed talking to Mamma Dell. I also talked to Carla."

"About what?"

"You mean with Carla?"

"Yes."

"I'm afraid I can't tell you that. It's something between the two of us that involves a third person. She may tell you if she wants you to know. I can't because the secret isn't just mine."

She smiled. "I guess I got told."

"No, not in the way you seem to think. Would you tell me something that was between you and Carla that wasn't yours to tell … yours alone?"

"No."

"That's what I mean."

"Did Mamma Dell talk about us?"

"Yes." He hoped she wouldn't ask him about that, and she didn't.

She stood up and touched his arms with her fingertips. "You're in training. You shouldn't stay up too late." She raised her face, kissed him softly, fleetingly and turned into the darkness.

CHAPTER TWELVE

Miss Martha paid her promised visit to Mamma Dell and found the old lady with her head wrapped in a shawl, sitting in the sun on her front porch.

"Good evening, you heartless old baby snatcher" was her greeting.

"Well, bless the Master if it ain't little Mottledy Marthy. Come in, Marthy … come in … set."

Miss Martha went up the steps and sat in a comfortable hide bottomed rocker. "So I'm still Mottledy Marthy to you, hunh?"

"Sure you is. Always will be. You was the oneriest young'n I ever seen in my born days. You was all mottled up …"

"Sure. You beat me half to death minutes after I was born."

"I didn't no such. Sure, I whupped up on you some 'cause you was too hardheaded to breathe.

"That city doctor your mamma sent for come in about that time. Caught me breathin' in her.

Miss Martha laughed. "Yes that was Dr. Curry. Every now and then he admits some of the things you did long ago are common practice now."

"Sure, like cuttin' a woman to keep her from tearin'. That just made good sense to me. I cut 'em right and left in my days, if they needed it. Cut 'em and sewed 'em back up. White thread on the black ones, and black thread on the white ones."

"What was that for?"

"So I could find 'em seven or eight days later when I got ready to take 'em out. Oh, I was a smart one in my time."

For half an hour they chatted away about old times and people they had known after a short silence, Miss Martha said, "Mamma Dell, I got me a boy."

Mamma Dell let her expert gaze run over the hearty figure, "At your age?? Well, you'd never know it just to look at you. Who's the daddy or do you know?"

Miss Martha turned pink. "Look, I'm bigger and younger'n you and I owe you a few for that whaling you gave me. Don't push me."

Mamma Dell wheezed with mirth. "All right. Tell me 'bout your boy."

"He lives right across the ravine from you. John Sidney Grahame. I've adopted him, sort of."

Mamma Dell sat up and her old eyes still sharp and steady, snapped to Miss Martha's. "Unh ... *hunh*. So that's what this here visit's about."

"Partly. I've been wanting to see you anyhow."

"I reckon you want to know about Delani?"

"That's right. I want to know everything about her from the cradle to now ... and mind you, don't skip anything."

A gentle sweat broke out on Mamma Dell's bronzed brow. "Oooowee, Martha. It's done come and I been knowin' it would for a long time." She took considerable time to get a cheroot going. She sighed and sat back. "You know, some years ago I made a solemn promise and I had my hand on the Bible when I made it. I was *never*, the longest day I lived, to make any statement about Delani and where she come from. If I did he would have me killed just like he would any sheep-killin' dog and never look back. See what I'm up against?"

Miss Martha knew that Mamma Dell ordinarily feared neither man nor devil. That this could concern her was the most amazing thing about the story.

Mamma Dell tapped the ash from her cheroot. "I'm an old woman, Martha, and I've had mine. I ain't here forever and as far as I'm concerned if it was only me, I'd put that child where she belonged tomorrow. The worst threat he made was that somehow he'd get her too, if I tried to do anything that would keep her from bein' raised as a Negro or if she tried to marry anyone but a Negro."

Miss Martha sat back in her chair, a little faint. "What you say doesn't shake me like what you haven't said, Mamma Dell."

"Like what, honey?"

"A lot of things. A white man told you that. A white man made you put your hand on the bible when you took your oath. He had you with a Bible under your hand and a gun at your back."

"No, you're a little bit wrong. It was a knife. He likes knives. He had used it before and he'd of used it that night without turnin' a hair. He'd still do it."

Miss Martha nodded and fished in her purse for a long brown cigarette. She lit it and sat back. "I'm not a fool and I don't believe in charging in the dark. I've got to protect you and her. Is there anything you can tell me without giving yourself away?"

Mamma Dell thought for a long time. "Well, reckon there is but what you're gonna do?"

"I'm goin' to parboil that leprous son of a bitch. I'm going to ruin him. I might even blast a hole in him myself." Her face was red with fury.

Mamma Dell looked at her carefully. "You know, you always a headstrong heifer. As bull headed as they come with too much money and too much time on your hands. Think about it well before you tie into this man. He's killed three men. He killed one woman but nobody but a very few knows about that and he didn't use no knife. He just drove her into an early grave."

Miss Martha went pale. "Would he own damn near half of Konka County?"

"He would ... he does."

"Owns the Johnstown Shipyards?"

"He does that."

Miss Martha sank back with a gusty sigh. "Damocles Osterbanns."

"All right." Her jaw was axe-hard now. "Without mentioning any names or places tell me a story about a man like Damocles Osterbanns."

Mamma Dell told the story.

CHAPTER THIRTEEN

"Imagine finding you here" trumpted Miss Martha, as she walked into Whitley's seldom used office.

Whitley grinned. "I do it occasionally, just to keep up a sort of gesture of independence. I handle a case once in a while."

"Hell, I got one for you to handle. I'm askin' you because you know all the different ways to cut legal corners and to pull off "Blackstone bull-doggery. I can sit down, can't I?"

"Oh, sure. You blow in here with so much wind and bluster I forget my manners. That's the client's chair."

"I'm a client. I'll take it. Now, the first thing I want to make plain is that the first time you mention how expensive this might me, I'm going to clout you one in the kisser. I got the money and I don't want any horses spared. I don't know how you're going to do it, but I'd imagine it would involve hiring the very best detective agency in the area … New Orleans probably."

Whitley's narrow sharp face looked expectant. "You sound serious."

"I was never more so. I want information, a lot of it. I don't want doings with any gumshoe. You handle that. Trouble is, Whit, I can't tell it all to you."

"Can you tell me what you want, without telling me all?"

"Well, in a manner. Let's see, you know Damocles Osterbanns, don't you?"

"I've heard of him. I don't think I'd care to know him."

Her eyes snapped. "You might find yourself rubbing up against some pretty slimy customers before this is over."

"Not me. I've handled cases like this before. I know just the man and I, like you, will stay way out of it. Now, some details. I take it it's something to do with Osterbann."

"Correct. I want a dossier on him a foot thick. I want his financial standing, I want what he eats for breakfast. I want the women he keeps around for the usual thing. I want the size of his shoes and if he wears drawers. In short, I want everything he ever did, ever thought, or ever misses doing ... the works."

"All right. Now on what particular phase of Damocles Osterbanns do you want dug into most?"

Her jaw went hard. "His wives, their deaths, ages, names, where from, living relatives, if any. Most especially do I want information on the third and last wife and *any* children, if there are any which I have reason to doubt."

He shook his head. "Now, Miss Martha ..."

"All right, forget what I said. Just get what I want and send me the bill."

"Any rush? This sort of thing usually takes time, you know."

"Well, No, I guess not. No! No rush. Just don't let the grass grow up between your toes."

"Do you want reports in piece meal, or in a lump?"

'I leave that up to you. If something comes in that might, well, Hell, I don't know. If you think I should know about it, give me a call. Oh, I particularly want to know how sound he is financially. If possible, I want to ruin him."

Whitley's eyes burned. "Damn, but you've got me in a fever of curiosity."

"Don't let it get you down. You'll be glad you had a part in it if it all comes out right. And another thing. I don't care that Judson

Markey has made you a working vice president, my business gets taken care of, hear?"

His eyes narrowed. "How did you know that? It hasn't been made official yet."

She chuckled. "I know a lot of things that'd cause a spotty exodus around here if people knew about it. I got my ways." She swept out and left him shaking his head.

Judson Markey had discovered something that both annoyed and pleased him. He discovered that Markey Associates Chemicals Incorporated could and would go along smoothly after he had drawn his last check. While he was sick nothing bottle-necked and then there was the added matter of old Northrup's plastic that had the lab in a tizzy because of the way it tested out. There seemed nothing it couldn't do, and its strength when moulded according to its inventor's specifications was astounding. Already the Navy had an ordinance officer on location supervising preparations for some tests.

Markey felt pressed into discussing his changed attitude with Dr. Forrest. There was a puzzled crease between his eyebrows. "Ever head of a man just turning the whole book over, not just a new page? He shrugged and lifted his hands. "I don't even know how to say it right."

Dr. Forrest, born nosey, was up on most things in the community without anyone being aware of it. At the moment he was, in a manner of speaking, looking down Markey's throat, but instead of twitting him, he chose to appear wise. "You mean everything looks different now. The green greener, the reds redder, and all other preceptions deepened and polished."

"That's what I mean, although what you mention are just symptoms. Does a close brush with death change a man's whole perspective?"

"It could if the man was more than usually sensitive. To some it wouldn't mean much. To a man like you, it might mean a great deal. You'd never thought much of death in cold black and white terms before. Once a man does, there are many values might even undergo a shocking shakeup." His beady eyes sought Markey's, but the other was looking broodingly at the floor.

"Yes. That's exactly what I mean. Making money, all of a sudden, seems so far away and so ... well not unimportant but not the flaming beacon it once was. The way I feel now and the way I lived before wouldn't sit in company five minutes. I find that my associates have brains, and I'm now willing to let the muse them. Before I hovered around, fretting and carving off this little roughness and that."

Now I discover I'm not much of a family man either. I sure have a couple of prizes as children, and another one as a wife."

"I think you're too harsh on yourself there. Any man who has to meet competition head on in the marts should be relieved of some of the responsibilities of the home."

"You've treated Esther, haven't you?"

"Yes."

"What do you think about her?"

Dr. Forrest grinned. "Can you take it?"

"I already have. I just wondered if you knew."

"Of course I know. A neurotic with ingrained food faddism. She got her natural drives cross ways, the current and now none of them are directed amidships, if you follow me. If they were then she'd probably be in demand at cocktail parties where you'd leave early or get tiddily. She'd drink just enough to lower her inhibitions and raise her skirts. She'd be circumspect because she wouldn't want to upset her position in the scheme of things. She enjoys being the wife of the president, and she might play but she wouldn't dump the bucket. As it is, her directions got changed.'"

"I think I prefer the last one you mentioned," growled Markey, frowning. "My own drives have begun to get straight and I find that the flesh has renewed its attractions."

"It should. Carla Smith could change any mind not atrophied."

Markey flushed violently. "Damn … is it common gossip?"

"Oh no. I doubt that more than three know about it. You, she young Grahame, and me."

"Whitley knows."

"Then you're well off. I've been accused of having a suspicious mind, leaning toward dirt. I don't deny it. I also know enough on the citizens of this town to cause mass consternation if I'd talk. I don't talk. Neither does Whitley."

Markey wrung the old man's hand "I've just started living after fifteen years of hibernation. I even find that people are pretty fine, with certain exceptions. Of course, you have to real- ize that before living can be anything but rote existance."

It was Thursday and Markey was nervous and had trouble ordering his thoughts. He summoned Whitley to his office.

"Whit, what's on for the rest of the week?"

Whitley grinned. "Miss Walker couldn't tell you?"

"I didn't ask her."

"Then you must have some reason for asking me."

Markey laughed shortly. "Well, to tell the truth, I was think- ing of taking off. I suppose I wanted you to tell me I couldn't, if there is any good reason why I shouldn't."

Whitley sat down and lit a cigarette. "Look man, you're the man with the mink stones around this place. Who's to tell you you can't take off?"

"It's not that. In my frame of mind. I just might go loping off when I'm really needed. I don't want to go overboard with this new sense of freedom."

"Take off. That Northrup deal doesn't come up until next week ... the contract negotiations and such."

"What about the suggestion program?"

"I can handle that. I took over when you were laid up. I've been carrying on."

"Yes, but you're my legal man. You shouldn't have to worry about such trifles."

"Products suggestions were never trifles here and you know it. Also, my legal duties are routine and young Jackson needs the practice. He'll never be able to find an opinion until he gets the smell of books on his hands. Too, if I'm to be a working vice president I better be shunting more work his way and start boning up on being an official."

"That's right. Okay, Whit. Off I go. You take over and you've got my backing all the way up to outright stupidity."

"Thanks Jud. Have fun. Y'all." He chuckled at Markey's flush and left the office.

Carla Smith would have felt a great deal worse over her own status had it not been for Delani, who moped quietly and whose face wore a sad set cast. Carla waited for some word from Markey, but none came. When she thought of what there was on the credit side of the sheet it seemed pitifully little. A look, the shock that had touched them both when their hands made contact, so many things which might mean much or nothing. She could not make the first move. She writhed with embarrassment when she thought even of accepting his admiration. To make a move was unthinkable. She had considered running out of gas again, but that would be so palpably a maneuver that her soul shrank from its performance. He knew, just as surely as she knew, but did she. She thought and hoped but she didn't know.

Mamma Dell nodded and came into the room to take a chair. "Not a word from him?"

Mamma Dell lit a cheroot and looked at her daughter shrewdly. "You know, give you half a chance and Mister Bigshot Markey's gonna be a handful of pull candy."

"Don't call him that. He's not that way at all."

"Just the same, I think I know you. You been too close to yourself. How many men you had in your life?"

"Two."

"That's what I mean. You know what it is, and yet you ain't no loose woman."

Carla's eyes had a faraway look in them. "Only one, really."

"The other'n was just a quick deep breath caught while you was runnin'?"

"Yes. Something like that." Carla faced her mother.

The phone in the hall rang shrilly.

"I'll get it" said Carla, pulling her robe together.

She went into the hallway and lifted the receiver. "Hello."

"Carla?"

"Yes." Her knees turned to water. It was *him*.

"Don't you think it's about time you ran out of gas again?"

A sob caught in her throat and for a wild fearful two seconds she was afraid she wouldn't be able to answer. Finally she got it out. "I think it's past time."

"Tonight?"

"Yes sir."

"Soon?"

"In an hour."

"Fine. The same place. Drive in and put your car under the little shed at the north side … just in case. Understand?"

"Perfectly."

She walked back into her room in a daze and turned her eyes to Mamma Dell who nodded wisely. "It was him."

"Yes!" She shivered. "Now I'm scared to death. Oh, Mamma Dell, what'll I *do*?"

"Up to now" averred Mamma Dell drily, "you been follerin' your nose. Seems it's a pretty good compass."

"You don't advise against it? Where's your maternal resistance against such a thing?"

"Never had any" snapped Mamma Dell. "I know too much about people and nature. I know you're my daughter and give or take a little one way or another, you ain't any different from many another. If I told you nay you already got ten outs thought up, so why waste my time? Treat him right, daughter, and he'll treat you right. You're kin to me, remember. Make this a night he'll never forget as long as he lives. Life ain't lined up like you want it I know, but them that beats the game is them who does the best they can with what they got. Nobody's gonna make the world over. You're colored and he's white. The world won't forget it, but you can make *him* forget it."

"Hello." He stood in the lighted frame of the doorway, his nerves jumping like wounded muscle.

"Hello," she quavered and stepped through the doorway, as he moved to let her pass.

She wore a summer weight nylon so near the color of her skin that Markey's heart thumped wildly. For a moment it seemed that she wore nothing. Her body, as it slipped slickly beneath the clinging fit of the material, was a fable in cream-bronze. Her breath was shortened, her lips slightly parted, and her eyes pools of dark hunger.

"Dinner is served" he choked.

"Not fish this time" she said lightly, laughing nervously.

"No fish. Steaks. I hope you like yours rare."

"I like steaks any way at all" she breathed and allowed him to seat her. The living-bed room had been redone and curtains drooped across the windows. The light was dim and on the table were two slim white candles. In the center of the table was an ashtray of water in which floated a single white camelia. It was large and so delicately formed as to resemble wax. She took in all these things at a glance and the turmoil increased.

They ate desultorily without appetite, paying more attention to the iced bottle of champagne that stood in an ice bucket close by.

When they had finished he led her to a couch and lit a cigarette for her. He served brandy in large pot snifters, then taking a deep breath plunged. "Carla, I've had a great deal of time to think. Maybe this is no good. One thing is certain. It isn't fair to you."

"Don't you think I've thought over all that a thousand times?"

"I suppose so. My point is, I don't want you to feel that I'm pressuring you into anything. I haven't forgotten that first time and I never will. I'm not a man easily impressed. I was sunk long before I swallowed that bone. I can't help it, but I do have enough principle to see that this is a pretty one sided thing. I can't offer you the things you have a right to expect. I haven't the guts to throw up everything and make another start somewhere else."

"Do you, for one moment, think I'd allow any such thing? Mr. Markey there is such a thing as a woman being too much to a man. She could make things so difficult for him that soon he'd begin asking himself if she was really worth it." A sob shook her. "I think I'm her because, like you, I was sunk before you swallowed that fishbone. I'm here because I want to be. I know your conscience is probably pricking you, but remember that I'm a mature woman, not a child. My eyes are open and I don't think you could think of anything I haven't already considered."

"And you made it all right with yourself?"

"I wouldn't be here if I hadn't."

He sighed. "Like you say, I suppose it's conscience ..." He looked at her suddenly and what he saw turned his will to water. She had laid her head back on the couch and her eyes, wide, damp and slightly oblique seemed to engulf him. They drew him so irrisistably that he felt a flit of fear. Closer and closer until he could see the fine sheen of her silky skin and the perfection of her full lips. Her tongue slid across them, leaving them aglow and ready. The touch of his own on their satiny surface was a shock. His heart hammered loudly and his arms went about her. Her eyes closed and her body became a flexible reed that bent to his every demand Her mouth was a well of delirious wonder and her jaws slackened, availing him of the entry he feverishly sought, and he went wild. She was warm and quiescent beneath the urging of his strength. Her breasts were promontories that stung his chest with their firmness. Her waist was narrow and the rich bulge of her hips so smooth and round made his head ring tinnily.

Their embrace was a meeting of nature's urges and in no way did she reject him. He released her and stood up, half fearfully, but she seemed to anticipate him and was standing also. He cut out the light, and hand in hand they walked across the room.

Judson Markey had known women. During his youth he had been a man of much charm and used it to the limit, but he had never known a woman like Carla. In the darkness of the cozy room, she lost her shyness and Markey could sense the magnificent abandon that was building up, taking him along without volition. She was a clinging, shockngly, sweet sabaryte, and with the disappearance of shyness there arose the deep mating song which provided the setting for her part of the golden bronze priestess, the approach to woman's mightiest mystery.

She was a tidal wave of desire and in her wake, Judson was dragged along, himself transformed into another being, taken to another world. His muscles long untested, reasserted their strength and now she was a smooth silken goddess in his arms. Hungry with nature's most powerful urge. The same hunger rose in him until at last he was not a master of a corporation, but man as fundamental as his earliest beginning, and she was his mate.

Later the moon rose and cast a lance of gold across her magnificient middle, revealing the exciting quality of her skin and the structure that now seemed twice as seductive.

He placed a gentle hand on the proud lift of her left breast, and felt the tremor that went through her.

"Never before …" It sounded like a benediction. "Never before in all my life."

She turned and held him close. "But from now on … *for the rest of your life.* I'll be the part of this that I provided."

"You provided it all" he answered profoundly. "This is really not me. When you're gone I'll be Judson Markey again."

"Don't say that" she chided, her lips touching gently, making him hungry again. "Do you think I could be this to any one else? Do you deny your own part?" She shivered and arched herself against him. It was repeated, like an echo. "Never … never to another man."

"I hope not. God … I hope not."

"Not for anyone else, never." Again the promise giving shape and structure to the future, and he was satisfied.

The moon shone richly on the luxurious length of the thigh that reached to possess him again.

CHAPTER FOURTEEN

"Well, your uncle's going out to my place tonight to hang this picture" said Miss Martha, in her brassy contralto. "I'm feeding him and giving him all the gin he can drink ... afterwards. Want to come?"

John Sidney shook his head. "Thanks Miss Martha, not tonight. I've got some home work, and ..." He paused confused.

She nodded sagely. "Sure. Well, don't expect us back at any decent hour. I might even make him take me to eat seafood at Gulfport. Can't ever tell what I might do."

They left and John Sidney sat thinking. Today he had deftly avoided Patti. He had no real respect for her. She, in her boldness, had erased the respect for women which he gave out automatic deference to their sex. Still, he would not harm her if he could help it. He was as careful of her, physically, as he could be. He shrugged angrily and another thought struck him. Delani ... He hadn't thought of her at all tonight. His spirits descended and stopped at the bottom with a thump. What was the matter with him? Was he, after all his stout declarations, a man of vacillating loyalties? A vision of her rose before his eyes. Her eyes, large, limpid and calm ... or slitted with enthusiasm and mirth. The exacting sculpture of her face with lush inviting lips, delicate patrician nose, the nobility of her features ... He got up and walked in a short sharp circle, then without stopping went out of the room, through the back door and into the yard.

She was there, her long legs bare, her torso wrapped in a white woolen jacket against the bite of the night air. He approached and looked down at her without speaking.

She looked at him, and for a moment there was a silence. She spoke. "It's not like it used to be." There was a thread of agony in her voice that cut him like a knife.

His nod was slow motion. "It's not like it used to be, and yet nothing's changed … not in me. You're still the world arched over my head. Any thought of you squeezes everyone else out."

"Maybe you just don't think about me as much as you used to."

"The fault … the fault must be mine."

She stood and now he could see that she was wearing only a little pajama-romper bottom. "Maybe it's because you don't know me, like you do her."

There was considerable shock in what she said when he realized what she meant. The greater part of the shock was the truth it contained. In the last essence, the only reason why Patti occupied his thoughts was because of what she provided. Delani presented no problem. She was still a mystery to him physically.

"I decided" she said slowly," that although we're both too young …" she shrugged lightly, "most people would say we're too young for anything but …" She sighed and raised her eyes to his, and John Sidney had a sudden wild impulse to run madly away from the spot. The corners of her mouth twitched and her eyes filled slowly with tears. "I can't stand it any more, John Sidney." She dropped her hands in a gesture of dispair, the jacket coming open and revealing a six inch trip of her to the tops of her pajama pants, an exciting, dusky starlit vista that seemed to him like the unclothing of divinity.

"I just don't know what to do. I suppose that's because I am young, but I do know that this … this whatever it is, has gotten too big for me. It's just … I …" With a sob, she turned, but he was too fast for her. He leaped and caught her, spun her around, he coat flying open, baring her from the waist up. There was a kind of despair in the strength of his embrace and as she had done once before, she seemed to become as soft as modeling clay, to cling and become one with him, the soft wonder of her body a heated extension of his own.

She lifted her face to him and in it was mirrored the aching want, the grief and pain that denial had cost her, and when his lips closed over hers, he knew that this time the river had been crossed, not in prospect but in fact.

When finally their starving mouths drew reluctantly apart, and they could in some manner appreciate the devastion that had been wrought John Sidney clutched her again, his hands beneath the jacket, caressing in a kind of quiet frenzy, the velvety skin.

Words poured from his throat blurred by emotion, incoherent, a litany to the burden of his heart. They were young and unprepared for such an onslought. She sobbed and caressed his face, her own weaving from side to side in a fever of excruciating love, not knowing what to do, what to say, feeling her own hurt … feeling his even keener.

Finally the conflagration died from its own fury and he felt stuporous. Delani was numb and deadened from the fearful deluge that had swept her. Finally out of the chaos words came to John Sidney. With the words came an impulse and neither of them had the strength to resist it.

"Uncle Hec isn't home" he said brokenly.

Without another word they turned and crossed the ravine. Like sleepwalkers they moved toward a certainty, neither being able to feel fear, concern, anything but the stimulus of the impulse. It was like two victims of a spell walking objectively toward a goal.

Inside his room John Sidney could see from his dim table lamp, for the first time, the full glory of this girl. He had known, he had sensed, but now with her standing before him her eyes glazed and only for him. He was her god and he enveloped her as a sun.

John Sidney broke out in a sweat of remorse. Not for what was to come, but a feeling that he didn't deserve her … that he was no sun, not even a very bright planet. Then he knew that to her he was and nothing else mattered.

A tender smile touched her face. "No one" she said softly. "No one but you and for you …" She lifted her shoulders lightly. "There's nothing … nothing I fear. Should I be modest? Should I be shy? Why? A little gurgle sounded in her throat, and with a sinuous move the jacket slid from her shoulders and dropped to the floor. All she wore now was the pajama shorts, and they were so thin she might not have had them on. "It's for you, all for you."

He took her tenderly in his arms and forcing calmness against the smashing charges of hurtling blood that hammered savagely against his ear drums, he held her for a space, drinking in the evanescent perfume of her body. Not an olfactory experiences but one o fall the senses. Her fragrance was a fact just as her hair was black and her eyes blue. It enveloped him in a rich fog and he thought he'd go mad.

"I want to be what you want me to be." She kissed with almost motherly softness. "Just be gentle with me."

John Sidney was gentle and his love soared to such heights that he felt disembodied, a man apart from the ravening madness that visited them, shook them with fearful violence and left them only dimly conscious. One thing struck through the rosy mists of their dreamland Most of the pain had gone. The pain and frustration, the confusion and dispair.

She turned on her side and put a hand to his face and turned it toward her. "It is a wonderful thing to find out you're *right*." She sighed tremulously and kissed him, the firm rosebud tips of her breasts tickling his chest as she moved. "Do you understand a few things maybe you didn't before?" A shudder shook her like a chill. "Oh, John Sidney, I thought I'd *die*. Mamma Dell says it doesn't happen like this … so wonderful the first time." She sought the curve of his neck with her face and relaxed.

John Sidney didn't trust himself to speak for a moment, then he said, "I understand so much I didn't understand before. The way I feel now I didn't understand anything before." He turned' and looked deeply in her damp eyes. "I love you, Delani."

She bit her lower lip, held it hard until at last her overloaded heart could stand it no longer and it slipped loose. She placed her face on his chest and cried with a quiet intensity that was more pain to him than if she'd had a noisy fit of weepng.

She raised her head and her hungry mouth found his and from that one kiss came the gradual development of the hunger recently quenced, but not satisfied.

At one o'clock Uncle Hec got out of Miss Martha's car and walked around to the driver's side. He bent over and said. "I don't think much of the idea, but after all the boy is here alone and he'll have to be told."

Miss Martha for once was subdued. "Hec, how'n hell did it happen? Dammit, do you suppose we got all our marbles?"

He smiled slowly. "I think it's one of the few sensible things I ever did. I go to hang a picture and look what happens."

She cast a heated glance at him. "All I ask of you is to be sensible about it. If you go getting on your pride and acting generally a male ass, I'll cane your tail for you."

He bent and kissed her. "I think I'll be a perfect spaniel."

She snorted. "That's worse. I'll kick you just like I would any other flea ridden cuff hound, Go to bed, Hector. It'll be your last time alone."

He grinned. "If you've heard I enjoyed it, you've been wrongly informed. Tomorrow?"

"Yes. I'll come in with the car and a truck."

He found them stretched on the bed. John Sidney's right arm cuddled her close and her head rested on his chest. He stood there for a long time a suffocating ache thickening his chest, making his breathing difficult. "What God has brought together" he said in an unbelievable voice. He shook his head and walking to a closet, took out a thin blanket and opening it, tossed it over them.

Delani stirred and opened her eyes, but John Sidney continued to sleep. Her eyes startled at first, saw the look on the big man's face and from then on for the rest of her life she loved him with an affection that knew no depth. She sat up, holding the blanket to her, fastening it under her arms. She smiled at him, a mature, flashing honey of a smile, that opened the portals of her soul and revealed to him vistas he had never dreamed she possessed. It was a rich verdant plain stretching to the end of the world. "Hello Uncle Hec" she said, her voice a throaty caress.

"I saw you" he said carefully. "I couldn't help it."

She tossed her head and her hair swung heavily, silkily and came back to rest on the smooth skin of her shoulders. "I must be a bad woman, Uncle Hec. I don't seem to mind in the least. You see, I saw you too."

"I ... er ... what do you mean?"

"When I opened my eyes, I saw all of you, in yours. It was a wonderful thing I saw."

He nodded slowly. "Tonight Delani, I've seen God at work and I feel like falling to my knees."

John Sidney woke, started mightily and muttered, "Good Lord, we fell asleep."

"So you did. I'll leave now and let you get dressed."

He left and Delani let a little gurgle of overpowering satisfaction escape her lips. She stretched and the blanket fell away from her. "He's so wonderful" she said, almost in a whisper.

"Yes" said John Sidney shortly. He glanced at the clock. "It's one o'clock. They might have the sheriff looking for you."

She slipped lithely out of bed and picked up her pajama shorts from the floor. "Will you hold them for me please?" She placed her hands on his shoulders and he helped her into her shorts like she was a small child, his heart hammering his ribs heavily. Then he helped her into the jacket.

"I'll walk with you to your house."

She cuddled close and kissed him softly. "Thank you, John Sidney, for this night, for a ..." She clutched him. "I don't know how to say it. You were here. Maybe you know."

He stroked her soft hair. "I know. I was here. I wouldn't want to have to say too much about it, either. Talk is so empty and it's only word."

He took her across the ravine and was startled to find Mamma Dell still awake sitting on the porch. There was no way around speaking to her. "I'm sorry she's late, Mamma Dell" he said quietly. "I hope you weren't worried."

"No son. I saw you go off together. I wasn't worried."

He hesitated. He felt he should say something else but he didn't know what or how to say it.

Delani with exquisite sensitiveness saw his dilemna, she turned and kissed him like the touch of a flower. "Good night, John Sidney, and thanks again."

He choked, but managed to say good night.

She stood on the ground and looked up at Mamma Dell, her hands in her jacket pockets holding it insecurely together. The old woman smiled. "You ain't hardly dressed for courtin' is you honey?"

With a bound Delani was on the porch. Another step she was in Mamma Dell's arms, weeping with wild relief.

Mamma Dell held her like a baby and crooned to her, stroking her hair. She began rocking just as though Delani was a baby who should be asleep.

Finally Delani sat up. "You … knew?"

Mamma Dell nodded. "Sure, I knew, honey."

"You're not mad at me?"

"I ain't one to get mad at the Lord's work. You knew long before the time came what was gonna happen and you still kep' on goin'."

"Why did you sit up and wait?"

" 'Cause I thought maybe you'd come home sorta distressed like, and you might like to tell Mamma Dell about it."

"I'm not distressed, but I'm glad you waited up." She told Mamma Dell about it, all of it.

"If you loved him before" said the old woman thoughtfully, "what is it you feel now?"

"I wish I could answer that. I really do. Words just couldn't tell the story. But he's mine now.

John Sidney walked slowly and thoughtfully home. He was nearly a legal man and inside he felt fearful and trembly. He had no way of knowing that under the same circumstances he might have felt the same way at thirty-five.

He shivered at the memory of them being caught cold by Uncle Hec. John Sidney felt a tremendous rush of affection for the older man. How many men could have performed like Uncle Hec … finding them nude and asleep, throwing a blanket over them to save them embarrassment. He had been forced to wake them, because they might have slept until the sun rose the next morning ... probably would have.

He stood in the door of the living room, his eyes those of a much older man, his face somber and thoughtful.

Uncle Hec tilted the gin bottle and took a deep drink.

"That was pretty swell ... the way you did it."

Uncle Hec grinned wryly. "I wasn't too sure how to go about it. It's a situation a man doesn't get much practice at." He sobered. "It's a picture I'll take to my grave."

"You mean her?"

"Her ... of course."

John Sidney sat down abruptly. "It's just about what I'd expect you to say. I felt it too."

"What about tomorrow?"

"That has me scared.

"I've found" said Uncle Hec with a scowl, that in times of indecision, it ain't a bad idea to ask the women. Especially if she's got the gumption Delani has ... or Miss Martha."

John Sidney raised his head. "Oh ... I meant to ask how the picture hanging went."

"It went. Then we went to Gulport and got beautifully and happily steamed up. Then came the question. I couldn't answer it, so I deferred to her. She didn't hesitate a minute."

John Sidney's brows contracted. "What in the tall blue world are you talking about?"

Uncle Hec blushed becomingly. "Well I guess it started about the time I'd mashed my finger the third time, and had used some ungentlemanly language. She observed, with reason, that I needed a keeper. I in turn observed that, well then, why didn't she offer to be my keeper. That was where I made my mistake, if a mistake was made, and I'm not persuaded that one was. I got down off the ladder and she was standing there with tears in her eyes so, softie that I am, I comforted her and she was a hog for comfort, and the comforting went on and on." Uncle Hec wiped his forehead that had suddenly become dewed with sweat. "Then a quiet fell upon us. We were uncomfortable in each other's presence. She suggested that we go get a load of seafood. That seemed the easy way out, so we went. All along the way we nipped out of a bottle. With dinner we had wine on top of several alcoholic appetizers. After dinner we had *creme de menthe* and on the way out of town started on the bottle again." He wiped his forehead again. "Ten miles out of town we turned around, went back and got married." Uncle Hec raised the gin bottle and drained it.

For some reason John Sidney found the recital amusing, and he roared with laughter, much to Uncle Hec's relief. His laughter finally under control John Sidney said, "But you couldn't. There's the license to get, medical examination ...."

"That is where your Aunt Martha was way ahead of me. Much to my surprise and not a little dismay, there was everything waiting for us. The J.P. with the license, a doctor standing by ... everything. I don't know when she did it, but she was sure looking down my throat. We move to her place tomorrow."

John Sidney gave this considerable thought. "I'm glad, Uncle Hec. You'll find out how glad I am when you find what you've been missing, not marrying, being a nursemaid for me."

Uncle Hec's eyes filled.

Next morning Miss Martha came in early, followed by a large moving van.

"The boy doesn't want to go" said Uncle Hec.

John Sidney came in and tried to explain the situation to her. "I finally discovered the top from the bottom of this girl business, Miss Martha. Delani is the top. Right now, I'd rather stay here."

Miss Martha, who saw a great deal, nodded wisely. "Well son, it's your decision. However, out at my place you won't be behind the iron curtain. I've two pickup trucks, one perfectly good car and a Jeep. They're yours from now on to use as you see fit. Did your uncle tell you that you now have an aunt?"

He nodded, took her in his arms and kissed her soundly. "I don't think either of you are as happy about that as I am."

"That's what you think. Now, do you still want to stay?"

John Sidney pondered for a moment. "Well, under the conditions as you described them, I guess not.

Miss Martha squeezed his arm. "Bless your heart. No one will shut you off.

CHAPTER FIFTEEN

M ark Carter was a meticulous methodical man. He made very few mistakes. For years he had been in the employ of one Damocles Osterbanns as a sort of general handy man, investigator and trouble shooter. In the industrial empire of Damocles Osterbanns there was a definite need for such a man. No one knew quite as well as Mark Carter that Osterbanns' empire was in dire danger of crumbling, because its founder was not a man to inspire confidence. This was not a factor of importance until under the financial pressure of expansion, Osterbanns had, like many another tycoon been forced to issue stock.

"I told you" Mark Carter was saying, "that you could go too far out. Now I find that some of the proxys you've been depending on are under strong pressure. I wouldn't bet on them. There's a lot of money involved and I've discovered that our whole structure has been thoroughly investigated by Marek Winston Associates of New Orleans. There's a big boil coming and it's getting hotter all the time."

He hated Mark Carter because Mark was one man who had never feared him.

"Who" the great man asked in a phlegmy voice, "is behind this investigation?"

"I don't know." heart. No one will shut you off."

"Can't you find out?"

"How, catch an operative and burn his feet?"

"Sure you have and would but you know how they work. Operatives do an assigned job. They know nothing" Carter's eyes bored into he thick man's face.

"I saved the worst news till last."

Osterbanns thick lips moved spasmodically. "How like you. Continue."

"I had to think a long time before I could make up my mind to tell you. I don't like repeating something that was told me in confidence without any idea it'd be repeated."

"Your ethics touch me" said Osterbanns woodenly. "Go on."

Carter's bony face tightened and his lips thinned. "She saved the life of the President of Markey Associates. It started that way. It has progressed. If I know Markey he'll start investigating. If he does and the old woman talks …."

Osterbanns spread out his thick hands on the expensive desk. "Stop her."

"How?"

The pale eyes came up. "Do I have to draw you a picture?"

"You'd better, and it better be one I can swallow."

"*Kill her.*"

"Suppose she has left a letter?"

Osterbanns hesitated only fractionally. "Kill them both. I said it years ago, and I meant it. I still do. Since that miserable little chippy of a daughter contaminated the Osterbann blood then it must stop right here. Take care of it."

"You still harping on that Turk being Negro?"

"I'll not discuss it with you. You're a jackal and always have been. What would you know of pride of blood?"

Carter stood up. He was long and spare, but rawhide tough. His face was a leathern mask. "Not enough of a jackal to do what you want. I think enough of my blood that I won't cause any of my forefathers to roll over in their grave."

"You're fired, Carter" rasped the thick liquid voice.

"Thanks. I needed that. The new president has already asked me to be his assistant."

"What new president. What the hell are you talking about?"

"Oh … he's now legal council for Markey Associates. Markey, the one I mentioned as probably the man who'll marry your granddaughter."

"Then Markey is behind all this then … it would tie in. He knows."

"That would seem to be the case, but I investigated that end of it. Not a word has been said around Markey Associates. I think you're wrong." He turned on his heels and walked out.

Slowly Damocles Osterbanns closed his heavy fists until the knuckles turned white. He knew Carter too well to accuse him of spreading malicious gossip. If Carter said the president was to be replaced, then from past experience, he knew it would likely happen. Carter had made one mistake, but it was a natural one. His informant, receiving only the scantiest of hints from Mamma Dell had drawn conclusions of his own, erroneous to the extent that he mistook Mamma Dell's hints to relate to Delani, when in reality it was Carla.

Osterbanns sat for an hour, his mind congealed in a clotted mass of dismay and hate. Pride was riding his back with whip and spur. And his granddaughter was in a position to consummate a marriage or at least a union that would continue Osterbanns blood in unworthy veins. This was the worst blow of all. There was the matter of the firing of Carter. There wasn't another man in the organization he'd trust with such a mission. He was not too old to still do so himself.

John Whitley stood before Miss Martha's house and gazed up at its incredbile bulk with the sort of awe that he might have accorded Khufu's pyramid.

"Well" she trumpeted from the front veranda, "you gonna stand there all day and gawk or come in?"

Whitley grinned. "This is the first time I've seen it so close. I've already been awed by you." He walked in and shook her hand "Got time for a little talk?"

"Plenty. Do nothing but talk and make love these days ... since I got me a new husband."

Whitley did a double take. "Married ... you?"

"Hell, yes. Any law against it?"

"Well, the law reads just the opposite ... or is it public opinion?"

"Shut up and come in. Want you to meet my husband."

They shook hands and Whitley took a chair. "All right to proceed with our business I suppose, Miss Martha?"

"Oh yes. I've briefed Hector. He knows all about it."

Uncle Hec went to a huge walnut sideboard and turned, "Build you a drink?"

"Thanks. Scotch and water, if you have it."

"You name it, we got it" snapped Miss Martha, heaving her solid bulk into a comfortable position. "What gives with business?"

"Well, first, I can't charge you anything."

"Why not?"

"Because I've discovered something that could mean a pile for myself."

"All right, give."

"Actually, I owe you something. In our investigation I found out plenty about Osterbanns. He's out on a limb stockwise and holds on by his proxys. They don't like him for sour apples and are just aching to give him the heave ho. So, I got the bright idea that, well, you see my father owned a good block of Gulf Industries shares, and I came by them when he died. I always tied them in with Louis Wilford who has a big block and we just went along with the rest. Neither of us knew much about the company's position. Now it seems we can ease Osterbanns out. If we can, I'm going to make a bid for president and also try to merge with Markey. That'll make it great for Markey and Gulf Industries too. I've been talking to stockholders and I can get proxies for fifty-three percent of the stock, solid. They're so burned up at Osterbanns that they jumped at the chance to give me their vote. So I can't ask you for a nickel."

"That's all well and good.

I'd alert Don Winterhalter and he'll make his deputies keep an eye on Mamma Dell's house."

Miss Martha figited. "Dammit, I don't like it. I think I'll hire a guard, full time."

Whitley shrugged. "That would cause a lot of attention.

"So what? I want those people alive. All of them. I dug out what I learned by virtually guaranteeing her protection."

Whitley said, "Why don't I get my New Orleans agency to provide protection? They can do it without a lot of noise and notice."

"A good idea. Attend to it, will you?"

"Yes Ma'm, I'll do that."

CHAPTER SIXTEEN

But Whitley dallied, thinking that time was not important, but he did not know with whom he had to deal, and Damocles Osterbanns was not an ordinary man.

On two occasions after the war there had been trouble and Osterbanns come out of it by the knife and derived an almost psychopathic satisfaction from it.

The only thing that slowed him down was that he did not know where the people he wished to exterminate lived and that he must discover. A quart of cheap wine bought him the needed information from a seedy alcoholic, of which Taretown had more than its share and Osterbanns licked his thick lips in simian satisfaction. First he'd get the old woman, then if the girl was available, her too. If the girl was not at the house he had, in the course of his conversation with the wino, discovered the whereabouts of Markey's camp. She would be there likely and that would be his next destination.

John Sidney had the gas line of the jeep pulled away from the carburetor and was blowing it out with lusty strokes of a tire pump. The Jeep had run crazily all the way to town and when he arrived at Mamma Dell's he immediately went to work on it. Gratified that the gas now flowed when he turned the motor over with the starter, he got out and started to reconnect the line to the carburetor.

Delani was an interested spectator and managed to get in the way constantly because it afforded her an opportunity to touch him. Idly she turned to face the front of the house where the open front door let a golden flood of light out into the yard.

She gasped. "John Sidney, *who is that?*"

John Sidney, stung by the urgency of her voice, spun lightly around and felt as though he had come face to face with a snake. The man walking toward Mamma Dell's house was a monstrosity on short bowed legs, gross, corpulent ... shapeless, and his eyes catching the gleam of the light, glowed green like a rabid animal. In his hand he held a thick bladed knife.

Damocles Osterbanns had at last lost that tight grip on sanity that had steered him past many an obstacle. Damocles Osterbanns was a madman now.

With a sibilant gasp John Sidney seized the girl and lifted her bodily into the seat of the Jeep. "Stay there and don't move. I mean it. *Don't you move a peg.*" With a leap he went through a side door and was into the front room in time to hear Mamma Dell's gasp of horror.

"Where is she?" He choked it out like a death rattle.

Mamma Dell stood slowly. "I'm an old woman" she said slowly. "Once you scared me half to death. You don't scare me no more. You'll never find her. You may kill me, but you'll never find her."

"He won't kill anybody" John Sidney stood easily just inside the door, his hands lightly on his hips.

A maniacal chuckle came from the cavernous chest. "I'll kill *you* and the old woman and *her.*

He lunged at John Sidney, slashing upward with the keen blade, but the boy stepped nimbly aside and smashed at the gross face with every ounce of strength in his wiry young body. His knuckles cut Osterbanns like a blade, but the man only grunted and John Sidney felt a cold weight in his stomach. He could beat his hands to splinters and this animal would still be slavering for his blood. He danced into the center of the room and Osterbanns, laughed rustily and slid the knife into his belt.

"With my hands" he grated. "With my hands I'll beat you to a pulp, then I'll gut you like a beef." He swung a hard left which John Sidney blocked with a shoulder, not realizing the strength of the man. The force of it carried him into a bed in one corner of the room as though he had been a sack of paper.

The bed collapsed with a crash and only a lightning leap saved the boy from being crushed beneath the great body as it hurtled through the air, trying to pin him to the wreck of the bed.

Osterbanns got up from the bed slowly and when again he faced John Sidney, the boy had a thick oak bedslat in his hands. He swung it and the sharp edge caught the man too high on the head, but the force was such that it nearly scalped him, tearing a huge slice of skin and flopping it over his left ear. Osterbanns roared and charged. Again John Sidney smashed him with the slat and this time it almost stunned him. He stumbled and fell in the front door.

The boy leaped to press the attack and tried to break the madman's back, but the slat caught air and curved, striking Osterbanns flatly instead of edgewise.

The big man, with surprising speed, without getting to his feet, lunged forward and caught John Sidney in a bear hug that would certainly have broken his back, but there came interference from another source. From the darkness of the back room came the spiteful crack of a .22 rifle and Osterbanns released the boy and stepped back. John Sidney, the breath squeezed out of him, sank to the floor.

The marksman had caught Osterbanns with his profile toward the muzzle. The bullet had struck his cheek and turned on the heavy bone, penetrated the lower part of his nose and shattered two of his lower molars. He was stunned from the shock but with a tenacity to consciousness that was inhuman, he stayed on his feet. He spat a gout of blood from his mouth and mumbled. "Girl ... not here ... Markey's camp ...." He turned and stumbled from the house still mumbling to himself.

John Sidney said, He'll go to the camp. Delani had the cheap single shot rifle that had been around the house for years, her face white and her hands clenching the weapon tightly.

John Sidney said, He'll go to the camp. He'll find ..." He stopped and glanced at Mamma Dell who still stood by the fireplace. The old woman nodded. "He was after Delani. He'll think Carla is Delani. She's at the camp."

John Sidney leaped through the door and out into the yard. Feverishly he fought the gas line back into position and screwed the sleeve nut up tight. "Mamma Dell" he yelled as he kicked the Jeep into action.

The old woman stood in the doorway. "Yes, Son?"

"Better call the sheriff and tell him to get out to Mr. Markey's camp as fast as he can."

She frowned then nodded slowly. "I guess so. Yes, I guess that'd be the thing to do. Can't bother about people's feelin's when that sorta man's loose."

"I'll try to have things cleared by the time the sheriff gets there. Delani give me the rifle. Do you have any more cartridges?"

"Three, I think" she said, sliding into the Jeep with him. "I'm going along."

"No."

"Yes." Her jaw was set hard. "You needed me in there a minute ago. You might need me again."

He smiled tightly. "There's no argument to that. Let's go."

John Sidney was not a reckless driver, but that night he tore from the hairychested little vehicle everything it could give.

Judson Markey lay stretched out on his bed, his soul at rest, his body surfeited and his mind as cool as the autumn air that filtered through the door that he hadn't closed.

Beside him, clad in nothing but a delightful expense of bronze velvety skin, Carla was also at peace. The tips of her breasts were now flattened and into the globular outline where half an hour ago they had been erect, exquisitely sensitive, telegraphing to her clamoring nerves his eagerness, presaging greater things to come.

"There's something almost unhuman in this kind of peace" he said softly.

She smiled and stretched like a cat. "I doubt if many humans ever know this kind of peace. It's the opposite of where we've been … the heights, the cold clamorous, steel edge of a joy that is almost an agony. Unless you can reach the heights then there is no peace like this, because it's the opposite end of the … *Oh, my God, what is that?*"

He stood silhouetted in the doorway, catching the light from the dim bulb that burned on the dresser. His face was a gory ruin and the torn scalp still hung limply over his left ear. His clothes were torn and drenched with blood and air bubbled through his wrecked nostrils that dripped a steady stream of claret.

Judson sat up with a suddenness that was painful, his eyes staring and filmed with shock. He saw the mad eyes, the bloodied face, the knife that was clutched in one ponderous fist. He saw the hideous wreckage that still stood as soldily on his great legs as though he had not been injured.

Markey felt his mind spin with confusion. The suddenness of the appearance of this apparition, the acute inconvenience of it viewed from almost any angle, as well as the menace that accompanied his appearance. Menace that was as palpable as concrete. Deadly, unmistakable.

The lips moved, cracking their icing of dried blood. "The blood of an Osterbanns ...." The head swiveled toward Carla. "You infected it in your mother's womb." The head swung back to Markey. "You would make garbage out of it. You would contaminate it further. A Celtic scab, garbage from an island of inbred lice."

He knew nothing of what the man was talking about, but of one thing he was certain, his presence meant death.

Markey was a man of great physical courage. He had always been a man's man and the hair that grew in a matted pelt on his chest was sprung from the glands of a man. He was also a man of decision. His alternative was not pleasant. He was unarmed and might die. The thought of this gross mockery of a man plunging that knife into the vitals of the woman beside him was something his mind could not endure. He gathered his legs beneath him, then suddenly launched himself forward like a projectile. He struck Osterbanns with all the force of his two hundred and twenty pounds of weight, crushing him back against the wall. Osterbanns was half blind, his lungs lacerated and torn from the prongs of the broken ribs, and still he labored mightily to break his opponent's back.

Markey then lost his head. He forgot the terrific power of those arms and back he went in like a charging bull. Osterbanns swung one fearful right that landed beneath Markey's right ear with a sickening thud, and as far as Markey was concerned the fight was ended. He was flung back to crash against the far wall, where he slid into a senseless pile.

Then Carla, her mind maddened by what she had seen, launched herself into the fight like a wounded lioness. She struck the big man breast on and rent his face to shreds, her nails slicing him like the claws of a cat. Osterbanns could not see her so terribly was his face torn, and now that his sight was gone a thread of fear chilled him.

As though a switch had been thrown, her mind shrugged off its fever and became coldly calculating. He pawed at his face and scrabbled along the wall, a torn remnant of a man but still dangerous. With a lithe spring she was upon him again. With a full armed swing she buried the sharp blade to the hilt in his lower abdomen. With all her strength she tugged upward as the breath of his gasping bellow fanned her face. Carla Smith had fought her battle. She had no more fight left.

Osterbanns, gutted like a prize porker on the rack.

At that moment Markey returned to consciousness, shook his head and sat up staring, his eyes still glassy from shock.

He staggered to his feet, pushed by an awful urgency that though active, still couldn't quite penetrate his consciousness. He shook his head again and John Sidney stepped into the room.

"Better get your clothes on, sir" he said forcefully. "The sheriff's coming. He mustn't find Carla here."

Markey beat his forehead with his fists. "Get her outa here, fast."

Carla was seated on the floor, rocking back and forth.

"Do you have some whiskey, sir?" asked John Sidney.

"Yes ... I'll."

Markey handed him half a bottle of bonded whiskey. He handed it to Carla. "Better take a good deep drink, Carla.

She nodded and gulped the straight liquor, drinking deep and long.

Markey swayed drunkenly on his feet, looking at her fabulous body drenched in blood from head to foot. He put a gentle hand on her shoulder. "You hurt?"

"No ... blood is his. I used the knife on him."

Delani came in with a bedspread which she cast over Carla. "We're wasting time" she said crisply.

Markey looked at her fresh face with stupified awe, as she helped Carla from the room. "Take her to the river, John Sidney" she ordered.

Five minutes later Sheriff Don Winterhalter appeared with a deputy and the reporter, Norm McLeod. The deputy took one look at the carnage and wheeled around and fell out into the yard, violently ill.

"Kinda young" apologized the sheriff mildly. "Not much bottom." He was stringy tall with a sandy drooping moustache.

McLeod leaned against the doorway and fought repeated waves of nausea. "I'm not young any more" he said complainingly. "And I guess I don't got much bottom either. My God, that man's cut to ribbons." McLeod had been in two wars and never had he seen a body so horribly butchered by human hands.

"Came in on me" said Markey woodenly, sitting with a thump in a chair. "Never saw the man before in my life. I did what I had to do."

"Who came in the other jeep" asked the sheriff.

"John Sidney Grahame. He came to warn me and got here late. He had a girl with him and I guess he took her out. Certainly no sight for a girl."

"Yeah" said the sheriff slowly. "Mamma Dell called me. Hadda been anybody else but her I'd of throwed a wet sheet on 'er and took her to Jackson ... with a story like that." He turned to McLeod. "He's Damocles Osterbanns."

McLeod stared, his eyes popping then pursed his lips in a soundless whistle.

The sheriff said, "You didn't know him, Mr. Markey?"

"No. Never saw him before."

"Well, it was your camp. He sure didn't have any business here."

"It's his knife too" said Markey pointing. "All I have around here is a couple of paring knives and a butcher knife."

The sheriff nodded. "Now, Mr. Markey, I'll want a formal statement, of course, but unless I miss my guess, you're shook to your teeth, you've been beat around. We'll meet at my office. I'll get it there."

Markey nodded. "That sounds like a deal.

"If you see the Grahame boy, send him back. I'll want to ask him a few questions about what happened at Mamma Dell's house."

Markey, soap and towel in hand, stopped. "Why not include him in the meeting at your office? I don't think he'll want to keep the girl out here any longer than necessary."

"Well, that'll be all right. Say, just who is that girl?"

"Do you think she had anything to do with it?"

"Oh no, I just …"

"Then I suggest that it's none of your business. I'll see you in town."

The sheriff took off his black hat and chuckled. "Well, I reckon I got myself told."

McLeod nodded slowly. "I'm afraid, Sheriff, you're going to have to be satisfied with about half a story."

"Ummmm, yep, I guess you're right.

McLeod grinned mirthlessly, refusing to look at the obscene blob on the floor.

Just as McLeod predicted, little came out at the sheriff's office that was not already known.

The coroner's verdict, death by knife wound of the abdomen. Justifiable homicide.

It was night and winter had set in. In Miss Martha's tremendous living room it was warm and cheerful.

Judson Markey sat in a chair. On his left was Uncle Hec. On his right, Miss Martha. Uncle Hec had made drinks.

"Before this past week said Markey, I didn't even know you people. You and your husband I mean. Your ... I mean John Sidney...."

"My son" corrected Miss Martha firmly.

Miss Martha smiled. "You're among friends, Jud. We know about you and Carla. Knowing your wife I can't say as I blame you. Go on from there."

Markey's face was thick with blood. "Well, he saved me again. He and a girl he had with him took off just in time. They brought her back in your Jeep. The sheriff suspects but who cares?"

"Right," said Uncle Hec. "You still haven't said what you came to say."

Markey squirmed. "No. I hardly know how to say it. I want to do something for the boy. I'd like to underwrite his education. I understand he's brilliant."

Uncle Hec nodded. "He is. Martha has been kind enough to underwrite his education."

Markey's face fell. He shook his head. "Let me do it. "It's the only way I know to do anything. He wouldn't accept a gratuitous gift and I'd feel silly trying to settle on an amount.

Miss Martha nodded. "Yes Jud, I know how you feel. Suppose we swap."

"How's that?"

"You pay for his schooling. I'll stand for his living expenses, he and his wife and any children that might come."

Markey blinked. "Children ... wife?"

"Maybe you'd better tell him the story while I erect new drinks," suggested Uncle Hec.

Aunt Martha told him the story and Markey listened, astounded. "Then Osterbanns must have thought Carla was Delani."

"Apparently. He didn't see Delani at Mamma Dell's. No one will ever know how he managed to get his information so garbled that he thought Carla was Delani. He'd never seen her, of course."

Markey shook his head. "I've lived a thousand years in the last week, and in the last year, ten thousand Looks like I'm just beginning to look around me and notice things."

"Want to make that trade?"

"Gladly. I think it's swell of you to let me. Just one thing. I don't want that boy to go to school on a shoestring. I intend to see that he has a new car and a charge account at a service station. He's no fool and it won't go to his head. He'll be able to handle a little success."

"Thanks, Jud. I feel that way too" she said, her eyes damp. "I'll tell him."

"Where is he?"

"He told me you said he could use your camp whenever the spirit moved him."

"Well, I certainly did. I'd give it to him if he'd have it. I had it all cleaned up and done over three days ago."

"Then I'd suspect him to be there with his girl. I think they've developed some very grownup ideas lately."

They sat on the couch, John Sidney in one of Markey's maroon silk robes, Delani swathed in one of Carla's.

She slid closer and nuzzled his shoulder. "I wonder why I've never felt self conscious or embarrassed around you."

She slid a long luscious leg from the confines of the robe and extended it for his eyes. It shimmered in the flickering red flames, surfaced with skin smoother than the costliest velvet.

His hand touched her with a caress that held an almost religious reverence. "I feel the same way," he said softly. "I guess we were meant for each other in a deeper than usual sense of the word." He frowned slightly. "I want it to be soon, the marriage, I mean. I know we're young, but we've gone a long way. I don't want any talk about us, and I want anything that happens to be intended, not accidental."

She slid into his arms and nestled there contentedly. "You do the thinking for us. I'm so full of your nearness ... the here and now of things that I can't do much thinking about the future."

He stroked her shoulder, slid his hands further and caressed the full exciting globe of one golden breast. She shivered and clutched him briefly. "Miss Martha" he said thoughtfully, "said not to worry about anything. To go ahead and make any plans I wanted to." He kissed her with a kind of desperation that twisted her heart painfully. Her eyes grew damp as she gave her body to his clutching arm.

He broke contact and held her close for a moment. "I've got to finish high school." Then college. Just the same, I want you there waiting for me every night."

"I'll be there" she murmured, urging herself closer.

"Oh ... how I *love* you!"

THE END

www.ingramcontent.com/pod-product-compliance
Lightning Source LLC
Chambersburg PA
CBHW052008240626

47153CB00008B/2790